Over and Over You

Over and Over You

Amy McAuley

A DEBORAH BRODIE BOOK
ROARING BROOK PRESS
NEW MILFORD, CONNECTICUT

A Deborah Brodie Book

Published by Roaring Brook Press

A Division of Holtzbrinck Publishing Holdings Limited Partnership

143 West Street

New Milford, Connecticut 06776

Distributed in Canada by H. B. Fenn and Company Ltd.

Library of Congress Cataloging-in-Publication Data

McAuley, Amy.

Over and over you / Amy McAuley.-- 1st ed.

p. cm.

"A Deborah Brodie book."

Summary: After visiting a psychic, seventeen-year-old Penny begins
having unsettling dreams about past lives in which she repeatedly causes
the deaths of her best friend, Diana, and Diana's boyfriend, Rick.

[1. Psychic ability--Fiction. 2. Reincarnation--Fiction. 3.
Supernatural--Fiction. 4. Dreams--Fiction.] I. Title.

PZ7.M478254Ov 2005

[Fic]--dc22

2004017549

ISBN 1-59643-017-6

Roaring Brook Press books are available for special promotions and premiums.
For details, contact Director of Special Markets, Holtzbrinck Publishers.

Book design by Jennifer Browne

Printed in the United States of America

First edition June 2005

2   4   6   8   10   9   7   5   3   1

1

I've been in love with the same boy for a thousand years. That's weird, especially since I'm only seventeen, and I can barely hold a guy's interest to the end of a five-minute conversation. Don't ask me how I've kept the same boyfriend for a millennium.

Last night, my mom threw a psychic party, mostly for her friends who need assurance that their futures will be better than their pasts. My innocent trip to the living room, to steal from the dessert and deli trays, somehow led to me visiting Margie, the psychic, too. I figured I'd get a far-fetched reading, laugh it off, and quickly forget about it. Turns out, I was right about the far-fetched part, wrong about being able to forget.

"We may not remember the people from our pasts," Margie said, "but when we happen upon them, it feels right. Circumstances bring us together in ways we can't understand." She flipped a red curl off her face and leaned closer. "Penny, the boy from your past, he is searching for you in this life, even though he doesn't realize it."

Margie may have thought her story was fun and romantic, but to find out that a reincarnated stranger is looking for me sent invisible feather dusters rolling down my skin. For all I know, the guy could be in Super-Saver with me at this very moment, squeezing the melons or choosing paper over plastic.

I scan groceries as they roll to me, lulled into a trance by the beep the machine makes whenever a product slides over it. My heavy head bobs with the rhythm.

Get to plastic divider bar. Smile at customer. Say "Hi!" in pretend, cheery voice. Ring up total. Kid strapped into cart screams for candy. Customer relents to shut kid up. Ring up total again. Customer scrounges within murky depths of gigantic purse for correct change she knows she has in there somewhere. Say "Thanks, have a nice night." Move on to the next customer. Scan groceries.

A chimp with a half-decent personality could do my job. I wish I didn't like money so much. I also wish I had a dad who liked money more than beer. Maybe then I'd have two parents who could take care of me, so I wouldn't have to work my ass off at a crappy job before trudging home to study and do homework. When I complain about it to Mom, she says, "Well, you can't get everything you want in life." Who the hell made up that stupid motto?

After work, I zip up my jacket and step from bright busyness into calm darkness. The energetic puppy persona I have to use at work seeps into the parking lot. I take a huge breath, inhaling a little part of the deep black sky. My shoulders slump.

"Penny!" My name echoes through the empty parking lot.

Squinting in the direction the voice came from, I spot three shadowy figures lined up beside a parked car at the side of the lot. The one in the middle is my best friend, Diana. I'd know her lithe ballerina body and maximum-volume voice anywhere. The identity of the other two is a mystery that I'm not too keen on solving. They're taller than Di, and built like guys. All I wanted to do after work was go home, take a bubble bath, and watch a movie. Something tells me my regularly scheduled program has been pre-empted.

"We're waiting!"

I sigh. Di can be the kindest, most serene person around. Or she can be the loudest, most obnoxious one. She blames her extreme personalities on being a Gemini. Yeah, sure, it all has to do with the alignment of the stars, not a chemical imbalance or anything. The only time she talks to me in that snappish way is when she's with a guy she's trying to hook up with, as if to immediately set the record straight that she's cooler than me.

"I'm coming," I call back. "Don't get your big grandma-underpants in a knot."

I'd do absolutely anything for Di. She's like a sister to me. The only problem is, sisters know where your frustration buttons are. And they don't mind pushing them. Sometimes I want to tackle Di to the ground and duke it out, like real siblings do.

We're alike in many ways, but where guys are concerned, we're polar opposites. I've never had a boyfriend, and she goes through guys like they're disposable razors. They eventually get dull and lose their edge, then they're chucked in the trash. In the five years I've known Di, she's had nine boyfriends, not counting the party stash of guys she keeps in reserve. Each breakup is followed by a guy-free period, and for the past three months, she's been single. Secretly, I was glad.

I step up to the car, looking only at Di's face. "Hi. What are you guys doing?"

"We were waiting for you," she says. "We're going to Ryan's to hang out."

Ryan. My gaze flicks side to side. He must be the dark-haired guy on Di's left. The blond one to her right is Scott McLean. I know because he's in my math class. All the girls think he's soooo cute. *Squeal!*

"We've got beer," Di adds, as if that'll convince me to leave with them.

The stiff collar of my shirt suddenly seems unbearably tight. Figures Di would show up with guys when she knows I'm dressed in my supreme-dork work uniform. What little makeup I wear to work wore off hours ago, my hair is a static-cling mess, and I probably stink.

"We have to stop by my place first," I say.

A hint of a smile tweaks Di's mouth. "Okay."

We get in the car, Di and Scott up front and Ryan and me in the back. Ryan gives me a smile as we're leaning toward each other to buckle our seat belts, and my stomach bounces up to say hello to my throat. Ryan is cute. Really, really cute. Instead of smiling back, I stare at the back of Di's head.

ZZZ

Ryan's older brother rents the basement from his parents. Since he's at work, we're hanging out in his apartment. Since his parents are out for the night, we're drinking.

"You don't talk much, Penny?"

I glance up at Ryan. He smiles with his beer bottle poised at his lips. The last time he came back from the bathroom, he sat on the floor, directly across from me.

"That depends," I say, shredding my bottle label.

"Get her another beer," Di says. "Pen is hilarious, but she gets nervous around guys."

I glance at her, annoyed, and notice she's now using Scott's lap as a chair.

How Di gets away with her slutty behavior astounds me. I figure it must be her hair. The way the light sparkles off it must hypnotize people; that's the only theory I can come up with. And guys are so easily bedazzled, it's frightening.

Ryan sets his bottle near my leg and clambers to standing. "You like Pink Floyd?"

I don't know anyone my age who likes the same music I do. "I love Pink Floyd."

"Come here. My brother has tons of CDs and albums."

Di's eyes and eyebrows suggest, in a not so subtle way, that I should get off my butt. I set my bottle on the worn brown carpet beside Ryan's and meet him at a huge CD rack.

"Have you seen the movie *The Wall*?" I ask.

"Sure, I have it on DVD. It's a great movie."

I laugh way too loudly, transforming into some alien girlie-girl I've never met before.

The drawer of the CD player whirrs open and Ryan sets a disc onto the holder.

When the music starts, Di groans. "You guys and your old-people music."

That's an ironic comment, coming from somebody who listens to classical music every day. Ryan and I smile at each other. Birds of a feather stick together.

We turn away from the stereo, only to find that Scott and Di are making out, and our beer bottles are in serious jeopardy of being knocked over by Scott's very large and very happy feet. Ryan creeps past the entangled bodies and rescues our beer in the nick of time. He sets the bottles on a table near the stereo and runs a hand through his hair, lifting it off his forehead. His bright green eyes remind me of the beautiful tropical ocean pictures in the travel magazines Mom pores over to torture herself.

"Would it be okay if I kissed you, Penny?"

I stiffen and glance over his shoulder.

"Don't worry, they're not paying any attention to us," he says.

That's partly what I was worried about, Di and Scott watching us, but there's one other gigantic thing that's bothering me. I've never kissed anybody before. Ever. Not even in middle school when we played stupid games like Spin the Bottle at parties. I went in the closet with the guy when my turn came up, but somehow I always managed to spend the entire two minutes talking, not kissing. I haven't practiced kissing a pillow or mirror or anything. I am so unprepared for this major milestone in my life.

I nod, and my brain cries, *No, shake head side to side, not up and down, dummy!*

Ryan licks his lips and leans toward me. I close my eyes. And then it's happening. He's kissing me slowly and romantically; the complete opposite of how I'd imagined a teenage guy would kiss. In the background, David Gilmour croons out one of my most favorite Pink Floyd tunes. My heart thumps hard and I feel ready to throw up. But it's mixed with the best feeling in the entire world.

Di made Ryan walk me home. Not against his will, he wanted to, but when she uses her loud voice, people tend to take action. I tried to convince her that I could walk home alone. She told me not to be stupid.

When Ryan and I got to my house, I casually mentioned, "There's my house," and we kept walking. We're on our sixth rotation around my block.

"Remember the Spirit Day we had in ninth grade?" Ryan says. "With the mud slide?"

"Wasn't that fun? At the end, Di and I looked like swamp monsters."

"You were wearing a sleeveless shirt. I thought you had good arms and shoulders."

Good arms and shoulders. That's a strange compliment.

Somebody must have forgotten to tell Ryan that guys don't notice me. When your best friend is a dancer with bedazzling hair, you grow accustomed to being her invisible sidekick.

I have clear memories of that Spirit Day, freshman year, and they don't include Ryan. I feel bad that he noticed me that long ago. I didn't know who he was until tonight.

He adjusts his baseball cap and takes hold of my hand. "Do you swim?"

"I can. I'm probably not very good anymore. Before my parents got divorced, I used to take lessons at the community pool during summer break."

"The pool on Nelson Street?" he asks, and I nod. "I'm a swim instructor there, Tuesdays and Wednesdays, after school. And I'm a lifeguard."

A lifeguard. That's in the same realm as fireman or race-car driver, as far as fantasy boyfriends go. I take a few seconds to picture Ryan in a Speedo.

As we approach my house, again, Ryan slows down.

"What do you like about teaching?" I ask, not wanting our talk to end.

"The beginners. Some of them come in too afraid to put their faces in the water, but by the end of the lessons, they're almost always swimming around like fish. That's cool," he says, and his enthusiasm makes me smile.

We stop at the end of my driveway. Mom's bedroom light is the only one on. Hopefully, she won't come out in her robe to remind me that I'm past curfew.

"There's not much I don't like about working at the pool. Maybe that I don't have as much free time as I'd like."

"I feel like I don't have enough free time, either."

Ryan adjusts his hat, pulling it forward and back. "If you get some free time, maybe you could come to the pool," he says, sounding as nervous as I feel. "We could swim a few laps or something."

"Okay. That sounds fun."

I have no idea why I said that. Swimming with Ryan would involve wearing a bathing suit. I might as well have agreed to flash him my underwear.

"Well, I should go inside," I say. Going inside is the last thing I want to do, but the longer our good-bye drags out, the more anxious I'll get, especially since I'm still on a high from my great first kiss. "I'll see you at school on Monday?"

"Sure. Your locker's near the library, right?"

"Right," I say, shocked that he knows where both my locker and the library are.

A firefly glows brightly near my front porch. For the first time in a least an hour, Ryan and I stand quietly together, tracking the bug's trail into my neighbor's yard.

While I'm waiting for the next tiny light to appear, Ryan gives me a fast kiss. "Bye, Penny. See you at school."

"Bye." I wave, jerkily, like my arm's forgotten how to work properly.

When I reach the side of the house, out of Ryan's sight, I do a funky dance, wishing I could let my happiness out in a big scream. I have way too much energy to go to sleep, even though it's late. I'll lie in bed, stare at the ceiling, and replay every second of tonight over and over in my head.

And, to think, all I wanted to do after work was go home and watch a movie.

◆◆◆ I'm naked. Not a cover-my-body-with-my-arms, embarrassed-type naked. This is a proud, lusty kind of naked that I've certainly never felt before. Silk and a thick blanket drape the bed beneath me. I'm alone.

Flames flicker at the ends of torches. Damp shadows caress the room's stone walls. People are coming. Female voices travel nearer, growing louder outside the wooden door on my right. They bustle into the room, a miasma of guttural speech. My ears hear French. My brain hears their words translated into English.

Two women draw me from the bed. Rough hands push, shove, and strap me into clothing I know to be my own. I'm whirled about.

Diana stands just inside the doorway, her white T-shirt and torn jeans soaked in blood. Torchlight glistens on the slick red trail that drips from her forehead to her chin. I'm nearly oblivious to the women fussing with my hair and clothing. A lump rises out of my chest, coming to rest in my throat like a jagged stone.

"Why!" Diana asks, her voice the breath of a ghost. Her mouth works, but I cannot hear what she is saying. I see her tongue roll as she admonishes me, and her white lips peel back in hateful scorn.

Flames lick her feet, appearing out of the floor like magic. Diana's head rears back. Silent screams bellow from her wide mouth.

Whimpering, I slowly wake up. My entire body is tensed. Pale beams of streetlamp light cross my blanket. My blanket. My room. The walls are peach and plastered in posters, they're not made of stone. I roll onto my stomach, too afraid to let my hands or arms dangle over the side of the bed. I'll never be able to get back to sleep with a vision of Diana covered in blood popping up behind my closed eyelids.

Think of other things: chocolate, cute furry kitties, Diana, blood, meadows of pretty wildflowers, oceans of blood, frolicking puppies, fire.

Damn. This isn't working.

Super-Saver closes
early on Sundays, but when I drag myself into the house after
work, I'm dead tired, as if I worked a ten-hour shift with
no breaks.

The phone rings while I'm taking off my shoes. My sister,
Kalli, runs into the kitchen on her long stilt-legs, sees me bent
over in the laundry room, and races to the phone to get there
before I do. I barely have the energy to hang up my coat.

"Peneeeelopeeeee!" she calls, stretching my name out like
an accordion. "Phone."

I sigh and trudge into the kitchen.

Kalli holds the receiver out, covering the mouthpiece. "It's
a *boy*!"

My legs feel like sandbags, and my feet are killing me, but I
run to grab the phone before Kalli can say something to embar-
rass me. She pulls the phone back at the last second, puckers up,
and pretends to kiss it. I yank it out of her hand and pretend to
whack her in the head with it.

"I'm telling Mom!" she squeals, galloping away.

I take a deep breath to compose myself. "Hello?"

"Hi, Penny, it's Ryan. I was wondering if you'd want to watch *The Wall* at my house on Friday," he says, and the words fly at me, like he's a speed-reading telemarketer.

When I realize that he's asking me out, I lean against the wall, lightheaded. Do I have plans for Friday? Do I have to work? I'm not sure. What's my name? Where am I?

"Sure," I say, not sure if I'm already busy, but Ryan is worth a sick day from work.

I catch Kalli spying on me from the stairs. My most menacing glare sends her scurrying to her room, but not before giving an imaginary phone one last kiss. She's thirteen going on nine.

Ryan and I get talking about school and new movies, and I don't notice that we've been on the phone a long time until Mom gets in from work. She taps her watch, which means I've been tying up the phone while she was trying to call home. She hates that.

"Are you feeling okay, Penny?" Mom says, after I hang up. "You look exhausted."

"I am. I hardly got any sleep last night."

"I'll make you a cup of my chamomile tea. In the morning, you'll be good as new."

◆◆
◆ Music swells to a magnificent crescendo. I stand at the center of a whirlwind of elegantly dressed men and women dancing, talking, and laughing.

A gloved hand waggles in the air, and Diana, dressed in a champagne-colored ball gown, appears out of a crowd of handsome men. She glides across the room like a silken cloud.

"Fun party, isn't it?" Di grabs my hand. With a squeeze to my fingers, she whispers, "Hans is here. I saw him arrive a few moments ago."

Hans. Sweat drenches my forehead and the insides of my gloves.

"Don't I look good?" Di says, spinning in a graceful circle to display her beauty.

Attached to the beaded bodice of her gown is one of those tacky sticker name tags that read, "Hello, my name is:" and the white space beneath is jam-packed with tiny lettering. Leaning closer, I see that each line is a name, and each name is smaller than the one before it, reminding me of the vision chart the eye doctor uses. Only the first name is large enough to read clearly: "Hello. My name is: Marie-Thérèse-Louise de Savoie-Carignan, Princesse de Lamballe." What a very long and unusual name Diana has.

When I back away and look around, we're standing alone in the stone room. The room with the gigantic bed. My heart races at the sight of it.

Torchlight flickers off Diana's face. "These dreams you're having are flashes of another life you lived," she says, tugging her hair loose from the fancy, piled-high-on-the-head style she'd been wearing at the party.

I take a seat on the end of the bed, sinking deep into the mattress. "Okay."

"But when you remember them, you're stuck seeing things through Penny's eyes, which includes her experiences and pre-conceived ideas."

I fall back onto the silky blankets. "Is that why you were wearing jeans and a T-shirt, and the walls in here are stone because I think all castles are like that?"

Stretched out on the bed, I wait for an answer. With each second of silence that passes, the tension in the room rises. I don't think Di is with me anymore. I don't sense her at all. But at the same time, I don't feel alone.

A frigid breeze tickles my bare arm, raising goose bumps. Invisible fingers of ice ruffle my hair and caress my cheek. When they fumble with the top of my corset, I manage to squeak out Diana's name, but she doesn't answer. Lifting my head slightly off the sheets, I see that the room is empty. A kiss so cold it feels hot envelops my mouth and pushes me back onto the bed, trapping a call for help.

When the kiss draws away, I lift my head and see a man standing at the end of the bed, his face hidden behind a golden lion mask. He lays a red rose on the blankets and slinks across the end of the bed, holding himself over me with his powerful arms. The mask lifts away, and though my mind gazes upon his face, seeing his beauty, my eyes do not. No matter which way I turn my head, I'm unable to see anything but a ghostly smudge where the mask had been.

Monday morning, I arrive at school still damp from a speedy shower, wearing two different colored socks and a wrinkled pair of jeans I found in the corner of my room. Mom was wrong about the chamomile tea All it did was wake me up to go to the bathroom. That, combined with another castle dream and a nightmare about Di chasing me around with her own severed arm, made it way too tempting to repeatedly smack the snooze button this morning.

I grab my books, hustle to my History classroom, and take my seat as the bell rings.

"Close call, Miss Fitzsimmons," Mr. Lamont says to me, shutting the door.

Mr. Lamont is the hottest teacher I've ever seen. He's the only reason I enrolled in Modern Western Civilization. I know he's a teacher, and I shouldn't scope him out, but I can't help it. Usually, I spend most of History class staring at Mr. Lamont's rear end as he scribbles on the blackboard. Or I time how long I can hold my breath. I can last over a minute now, and when I started I could only hold it for twenty seconds. That's something to be proud of.

Mr. Lamont writes "The French Revolution" on the board. I know all I need to know about the French Revolution, which is basically zilch, so I inhale deeply and watch the red second hand move around the clock.

"Louis the Sixteenth and Marie Antoinette." He pauses to write on the board again.

"She's the one who said, 'Let them eat cake,' right?" I hear Claire Wilson ask.

The second hand ticks past the thirty-second mark. I'm not even getting woozy yet.

"That would be the infamous quote, yes."

Yeah, whatever.

The second hand approaches the minute mark. My lungs burn. In the background haze, I hear Mr. Lamont talking about Versailles. I fade out of his lecture, focusing on the clock. When I think I'm about to die from lack of oxygen, I quietly exhale. My head floats around in a circle like it's not attached to my body. I catch sight of Louis's name on the blackboard in glaring white chalk. Why are we even wasting time on him?

"Louis was a fat moron who couldn't even get it up."

My palms throb. I unfurl clenched fists to expose a row of crescent-shaped marks left by my fingernails. Then it hits me that I just said something out loud, and the room is silent. I slowly lift my gaze. Everybody, including Mr. Lamont, is staring at me.

"Penny, I'd like to see you after class," Mr. Lamont says, and my cheeks flare red hot.

What did I say? I can't remember.

When Mr. Lamont's back is turned to the class, Moira Ezzo, the girl who sits in front of me, turns around to give me a wide-eyed look of shock. "That was amazing."

I swallow hard, unable to whisper back. I just nod, and she turns to face the front. When the bell rings, I keep my head down and pretend to be writing something in my notebook. People snicker as they walk past me to leave the room, but I don't look up. Then I see Mr. Lamont's dress pants beside my desk.

"Penny, it's not like you to be rude in class."

Am I sensing a hint of amusement behind his disappointment? Maybe I'm not going to rot in detention after all. I doodle a flower on the cover of my binder. "I'm sorry," I say, not sure what I'm apologizing for.

"I'm curious to know how you knew of Louis's"—he clears his throat—"ailment. Most people don't know that he was impotent for the first seven years of his marriage."

Oh my God, is that what I said?

"I did some extra reading on the French Revolution. I'd like to do well in your class, Mr. Lamont." I cross my fingers and pray that was just the right amount of butt-kissing to get out of trouble.

"I appreciate your interest in history," he says, giving me a smile on the way to his desk, "but you'll have to refrain from blurting out your findings during class."

How can I refrain from blurting out findings that I didn't even find in the first place?

"I promise I'll never do that again, Mr. Lamont." I hope.

"Pen, I heard about what you said in History," Diana says, cackling in my ear.

I stuff my math textbook inside my locker. "I think I blacked out, because I don't remember saying it at all. What if I have some rare disease where I blurt out stuff?"

"You think you have a disorder that causes you to hurl insults at dead historical figures?" Diana doubles over, cracking up. When she comes up for air she cries, "Christopher Columbus sailed big ships to compensate for his microscopic penis!"

"Stop making fun of me. I'm serious." It's way too hard to keep a straight face when your best friend is nearly peeing her pants right beside you. I crack up, too, and Di gives me a weak high five. "Thanks. I don't even know what I was worried about now."

"C'mon, let's go eat," she says, tugging on my arm. "I get to buy a treat today."

Di's body is her "instrument," which is why she eats healthier than any person I've ever met. It makes me ill. Every Monday, she rewards herself with a bag of chips, and then out of guilt eats only five. Sometimes I want to scream, "Just eat the damn chips!" But if Di ate them, I wouldn't get my free bag of hand-me-down chips, so I keep quiet.

"I should have skipped dance class the other night to go to your mom's psychic party. I'd love to know what's in my future," Di says. "What'd she tell you?"

"She asked if I have a friend named Donna or Diane."

Di grips my arm. "She didn't!"

"She did."

"Did you tell her she was right?"

I wriggle free of Di's bony fingers. "She wasn't right. Your name is Diana."

"Close enough," she says, excited. "What else? Tell me everything."

I could tell Di everything, if I wanted to. But I feel silly, talking about something that shouldn't be taken seriously. Nothing the psychic told me was even accurate.

I was in the spare bedroom, across the card table from

Margie, when she waved me over. For a minute or so, she just smoked a slender cigarette, filling the air with the scent of burnt mint, and said nothing. I squirmed in my seat and monitored the tube of ash that dangled precipitously over my mom's flammable tablecloth.

Eventually, she flicked the ashes into the ashtray. Tendrils of smoke curled from her nose and mouth as she said, "Honey, do you believe in destiny?"

I shrugged, wondering how Mom managed to finagle me, a skeptic, into seeing the psychic. Everybody else at her party was in the living room, sipping wine and playing dumb party games, while I was getting cancer from the clouds of mint smoke descending on me like nuclear fallout.

"Everything happens for a reason," Margie said. "Have you noticed this before?"

When I was twelve, Mom didn't have enough money to send me to my favorite summer camp. At the last minute, she sent me to a cheaper one. That's where I met Di. We'd spent our whole lives in the same city, separated by only four blocks, and we had to travel a hundred miles away from home to meet each other. It felt like we'd been best friends forever and picked up where we'd left off.

I wasn't sure if that was the kind of thing Margie meant, but I nodded anyway.

"Do you have plans to travel soon, Penny? Are you going away this summer?"

"I don't think so. I can't go anywhere because I've got a job at Super-Saver."

"No, I see you traveling," she said. "Do you know a girl named Donna? Diane?"

"My best friend's name is Diana," I blurted, accidentally feeding her information.

"There is another girl who is linked to you. I'm picking up a strong personality." Margie opened one eye only long enough to safely guide her cigarette to her mouth. "This girl is unique, set apart from almost everyone she knows. I see you take her black hair in your hands. You tie it in a knot," her hands acted out tying the knot and pulling it tight, "and weave the hair that falls to her waist into a braid. Sadly, a rift pulled the two of you apart. A rift that only time could heal."

The reading dragged on for another five minutes, and as soon as it was done, I jumped up to leave, eager to get back to the dessert tray before the brownies disappeared. The chunky bracelet on Margie's wrist bounced against my arm as she held me back.

"Have you ever tried to read someone?" she asked.

"You mean like psychically read them?"

"Yes, like that," she said, pulling me closer. "I can see many things about you, Penny. But I'll let you find them out yourself."

On my way out, I paused. "If I meet the guy you told me about, who I've been in love with for a thousand years, I'll know?"

"Oh, honey, you'll know all right. He's charismatic and attractive, in a majestic way. I'm getting the initial *U* in his name. Only the letter *U*, though, the rest is unclear." She pawed the air around her face. "The word lion is coming to me."

Her calm expression suddenly tightened into a grimace. I wondered what she saw, but didn't ask. I guess I'll never know.

"He has the initial *U*?" Di says, after I tell her the short version of what happened. "What's his name? Uterus?" The word *uterus* punches a hole through my eardrum. "I guess that means Ryan isn't your past-life lover-man."

"Nobody's my past-life anything. He can't possibly be a real person."

Di tugs a lip balm from her pocket and slathers on a veneer of sparkly gunk. "Who knows. Maybe he is real and you'll meet him when you're ancient. Like thirty."

Inside the cafeteria, we take our usual seats at a table we share with Amanda and Valerie, the girls we hang out with at school.

Amanda wrinkles her nose at me. "You look terrible. Are you sick?"

Great, in one day, I've gone from looking tired to terrible. At the exact same time a guy is finally interested in me.

"I've been having weird dreams that keep me up at night," I say, scanning the lunch specials board. "Plus I feel awake during them, like I'm only half sleeping."

"That's called lucid dreaming," Valerie says.

I turn abruptly at the unexpected response. Val is so quiet we sometimes forget she's there. She must know about lucid dreaming or she wouldn't have said a word.

"Do you lucid dream?" I ask her, and she draws a sci-fi novel away from her face.

"All the time. You controlled what happened in your dreams?"

"Not really. It was more like I was awake and thinking. But I knew I was dreaming."

"I think dreams are a way for our brains to tell us things we don't or can't normally think about. I have a dream journal beside my bed. If I write dreams down it helps me remember them and figure them out. And it makes me a better lucid dreamer."

Uh huh. That's all I'd need. Bigger, better nightmares.

I don't know how long I'll have to suffer through panic and euphoria every time I'm around Ryan. My brain function grinds to a halt, my speech patterns alter drastically, and my heart does whatever it wants. Di told me it takes about a month to get comfortable with someone, but I'm not sure if I can tolerate myself for that long.

To make movie night more like a real date, Ryan and I went out to dinner, and I sweated over my table manners the entire time. Having a boyfriend is going to be the death of me.

Ryan holds the door of his house open for me. I step inside and wipe my feet on the butterfly-shaped mat. This isn't the first time I've been in his kitchen, I ate lunch here yesterday, but his mom wasn't home at the time.

"Mom, this is Penny," Ryan says to the short, dark-haired woman loading plates into the dishwasher. "Penny, this is my mom, Linda."

"It's lovely to meet you, Penny," she gushes, extending her hand.

My hands are cold and clammy, like dead fish, but I slap one of them against her palm anyway, and she gives it an enthusiastic jerk.

"It's nice to meet you, too," I say, sounding like a frog with laryngitis.

"Ryan has told me so much about you." Linda releases her overzealous-mom death-grip on my hand. "He says you both have the same taste in movies and music."

I give her the polite smile I know moms love best. "That's right."

"Ryan loves music. He's a talented guitar player. But you probably already know that. And he's quite the swimmer. His dad and I are stunned by his lap times this—"

"Mom," Ryan says, laying a hand on her arm. "We're gonna watch the movie now."

"Sam doesn't mind if you use his DVD player, Ryan, but be out of his apartment before he gets home at eleven-thirty."

"I know, Mom."

Ryan's warm fingers slide around mine. With his mom muttering in the background, he tugs me out of the kitchen and opens a door in the hallway. The staircase ahead of us leads down into pitch darkness.

❖❖
❖ I'm sitting in History class. Mr. Lamont stands at the front of the room, waggling that cute butt of his around at the chalkboard. I glance around the empty room, wondering where everybody is. But then Moira turns around in her desk in front of me. That's weird. She wasn't there two seconds ago.

Leaning toward me, she whispers, "The crowd is totally crazy out there."

I boost myself up to peek out the windows at the back of the room. Smoke drifts past the windows, coiling through the air like a snake.

"What's the crowd doing?" I ask.

"Surely you must know," Moira says in French. "Who are you kidding?"

I think hard. "No, really, I don't know."

"You used her. She loved you like a sister and you used her in your treasonous exploits. Did you not care about her?"

In a way, I know what Moira's talking about, but at the same time, I feel clueless. It reminds me of the game of Hangman, when the word is nearly filled in but your brain can't quite put it together.

"Okay, we can play hangman if you want," Moira says, already slashing white lines of chalk across the blackboard.

"Hang her!" Mr. Lamont cheers from the other end of the board.

Moira taps the chalk impatiently. "It's a three-word phrase. Go!"

I choose the letter **Y**. Moira smirks and draws a circular head at the bottom of the noose. She writes the **Y** above the word so I'll remember I already chose it.

My next choices, **E, I, O** and **U**, are all correct, and when I choose the letter **N**, Moira spears me with an angry glare before filling in the fourth space.

"You'll never be hanged at this rate," she says.

"How about **D**?"

"Nope!" She attaches a stick body to my head.

The phrase is nearly complete. I choose **T**, and it's the last letter of the last word. When I call out **L**, hate flares into Moira's face and the chalk snaps. White dust flutters from her fingers to the floor.

Only one spot remains blank. I will not hang. "It's **G**."

"That it is," Moira says, grimacing in defeat.

The phrase reads: LIE, NO GUILT.

"So, what does it say!" Mr. Lamont calls.

"It says . . ." I stop in surprise. The letters in the hangman's phrase have rearranged themselves into one word. It now says: GUILLOTINE.

The vowels fade from the word **guillotine** and burrow beneath the board. Vein-like ripples surge toward the letters **Y** and **D**—my incorrect hangman choices. Red trails drip into the metal chalk tray as the vowels push forth from the board.

Moira claps her hands. "Would you look at that. It says YOU DIE!"

Wake up, wake up, wake up!

Without moving, I find myself at the classroom windows. Screams rattle the glass in front of my nose. In my peripheral vision, I catch a glimpse of blond hair, and then Diana's face bobs into view, with only a pane of glass separating us.

"Come inside. Something bad is happening!" I want to shout, but her face disappears below the window ledge before I can utter a word of warning.

To my relief, it bobs back up. It slowly inches higher and higher as if she's drawing up on her tiptoes. I reel backwards.

Diana can't be standing on her tiptoes. I watch in horror as her dismembered head, impaled on a pike, is paraded past the window—

I wake up pressed flat against the mattress, and breathe hard against my pillow a few times. A terrified moan slips past my lips. Another dream. About Diana. This is getting really bad, and I don't understand what my brain is trying to tell me. Di ticks me off sometimes, but it's not like I want to kill her or anything. Of course, if those feelings were subconscious, how would I know about them? What kind of person has dreams like this about their best friend? It's not right.

My alarm clock reads 2:36. I can't analyze my psychotic dreams right now. With my eyes shut tight, I breathe slowly through my nose and count fat, woolly sheep. By the time I reach four hundred, I'm too pissed off at the sheep for not doing their job properly to fall asleep.

3:02. I watch the ceiling fan go round and round, and listen to the mournful whistle of the wind.

Something strange is happening to me. It must be Margie's fault. The dreams started right after she gave me her "psychic" reading. In one dream, Di told me that the dreams are glimpses of a past life. There. That goes to show that Margie messed with my head and kicked my imagination into overdrive. But . . . that doesn't really explain my outburst in History. What was that about? I'm pretty sure I didn't have knowledge of Louis the Sixteenth's sex life squirreled away in my brain just waiting to get loose. And I don't know anybody named Hans. Did I make him up? Did I also make up the name on Di's nametag, Princess Mary de Lampball something-or-other?

I close my eyes. I see Di's head on a blood-streaked pole. I open my eyes.

Sleep is highly overrated. Who needs it?

3:27. I roll onto my back and massage my temples. *Think, think, think.*

Women speaking French, corsets, a castle, a guy named Hans, a bloody princess, Louis the Sixteenth, and my death by guillotine. What does it all add up to?

Bathed in powder-gray moonlight, the fan whirls above me, blurred to a circular, rotating blade. In my mind's eye I see the blade plummet, to sever my head with a swift and brutal *chop*.

How do you tell your best friend that you're insane and casually fit it into everyday conversation? Should I say, "In a previous life, I was the queen of France. My husband was king, but I liked a guy named Hans. And you were my best friend, Di. You were a princess. I'm not sure yet, but from what I gather, you were ripped to pieces by an angry mob. Yeah, I know it all sounds unbelievable, and I'm totally going Shirley MacLaine on you, but I swear every word is true. Well, I'm off to Biology." I don't think so.

I rub the back of my hand over my eyelids in a vain attempt to moisten the red, dried-out orbs that are my eyeballs. If I could lay my head on the cafeteria table and take a nap without being ridiculed or drawn on with permanent markers, I would.

Heck, I'm so tired right now I might take my chances. Maybe I'd look good with a mustache or unibrow.

Di takes delicate bites of vegetarian pizza. "You didn't sleep well last night?"

"I didn't sleep, period." Through the open cafeteria doors, I see Mr. Lamont hurry into an adjacent classroom, and it gives me an idea. "I'll be right back."

With pizza in her mouth, Di mumbles something incoherent when I race away.

From the doorway of the classroom, I peek inside. "Mr. Lamont?"

He glances up from his desk. "Hi, Penny, come in." Laying a smooshed peanut butter sandwich on a napkin, he says, "What can I do for you?"

With my every step toward Mr. Lamont's desk, my cheeks flare hotter. "I have some questions about the French Revolution."

"Great," he says, all enthusiastic. "Fire away."

I clear my throat. "Did Marie Antoinette know a guy named Hans?"

"Yes, she did. How do you know that? Doing more research, Penny?"

Whew, my cheeks just got even hotter. Thought it wasn't possible, but I was wrong. "Yeah, I've been doing research. Could you tell me about him?"

"I know a few things about Hans, but let's take a look in here," he says, hoisting a gigantic book out of his desk drawer. The pages flap noisily as he thumbs through them. "Here we go. Hans Axel von Fersen was a Swedish soldier. He was transferred to the French Army and also fought in America during the War of Independence." His finger skims down the columns of tiny text. "He was a close friend of Marie Antoinette's, and when she and the king tried to escape Paris after the Revolution, he drove the coach that carried the royal family. But the escape failed and the family was captured. I'm sure you already know that Louis and Marie were both sent to the guillotine."

Shudder. "Yes. I know that." My hands clench to keep from fanning my scalding hot face. "How close of a friend was he?" I ask, staring intently at the sandwich.

He coughs out a laugh. "Well, I'm not sure, I wasn't there."

I think I was there, you see, and they may have been very close, if you get my drift.

"But seriously," he continues, "there are books that say they were lovers and there are books that say they weren't. The French people made up many rumors about Marie because they disliked her so much. It's hard to know what's fact and what's fiction."

"Why didn't they like her?"

Mr. Lamont shrugs his broad shoulders. "There were many reasons. She favored her home country, Austria, rather than France. And during the first years of her marriage, she didn't produce an heir. The people blamed her because they didn't know about Louis's impotence. She was also the victim in a scandal over a diamond necklace and that hurt her reputation, even though she was innocent. And she had a very close group of friends that she spent all of her time with, which ticked off important members of the court. They said she had affairs, she gambled, she spent France's money like it was water. By the time the Revolution came along, she was already despised."

She was despised. Searing anger pounds inside my tightening chest, and I lean against the desk, trying to catch my breath. I want to raise my fists and scream that I was a teenager forced to marry a stranger. I was blamed for things I didn't do. I loved my friends. I loved having fun. I wasn't evil. Speckles of light dart in front of my face, and I clutch Mr. Lamont's desk to steady myself. My fingers sink into the soft mushiness that must be his sandwich.

Mr. Lamont's desk chair scrapes loudly against the floor. "Penny, are you all right?"

"I think I'm gonna faint," I whisper, as my peripheral vision closes in. I feel him grab my arms. He lowers me onto the padded seat of the chair.

His face hovers in my small circle of vision. "Do you need me to go get the nurse?"

"I'm fine." The blackness fades back, and then I can see again. "Can't say the same for your sandwich, though."

He smiles and dangles the flat sandwich in the air to peek through the holes my fingers made—clear through both slices of bread. "You're lucky I didn't take the leftover chili my wife told me to bring for lunch."

I push the chair back. My head is fuzzy, but I confidently walk to the door like I'm back to normal.

"Are you sure you're all right?" Mr. Lamont asks.

My gaze wants to roam around the room, but I force myself

to look him in the eyes and smile. "I didn't eat breakfast or lunch. I'll go get something right now."

"That sounds like a good idea," he says, wrapping his sandwich in the napkin. "I hope I answered all your questions about the French Revolution. Anything else you want to ask me before you go?"

My mouth opens to say "nope," but then one more question pops into my head. "Whatever happened to Hans?"

Mr. Lamont tosses the sandwich in the garbage can. "It's pretty gruesome. Sure you want to hear it?"

I nod after a couple of seconds of hesitation.

"Hans lived through the French Revolution. But during the Swedish Revolution, he was killed by an enraged mob."

All the saliva in my mouth seems to dry up at once. "He was? Wasn't Marie's best friend killed that way, too? The Princesse de Lam . . . ?" I pause, struggling to recall an image of Diana's name tag in my mind.

"Princesse de Lambelle?" he says, and I nod vigorously. "Yes, she was killed by a mob, too. Her severed head was paraded past the queen's jail window." Mr. Lamont crosses his arms and gives me an impressed grin. "You sure know your history. I may have to give you extra credit."

I laugh, like I know he expects me to, and hope it doesn't sound phony.

"I guess it wasn't good luck to be best friends with Marie Antoinette, eh?" he says.

I guess not.

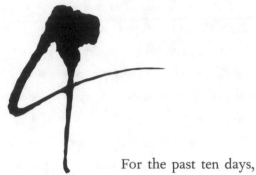

For the past ten days, I've been nightmare-free. Maybe all the Marie Antoinette garbage is finally finished. I can only hope. Lack of sleep was taking its toll on my appearance, and I don't have much room to slide backwards on the beauty scale.

After school, I drop my backpack in the middle of the laundry room.

"Great, I'd love that," Kalli says in the kitchen. "I will for sure. I'm so excited."

What's the dimwit excited about?

"I miss you lots, too. Penny just got home," Kalli says, and I perk up at the mention of my name. "Penny! Dad wants to talk to you!"

I jog into the kitchen and make slicing motions across my throat to signal "Shut up!"

"Dad, I must have heard wrong. She's not here." Kalli sticks her tongue out at me.

"What did the jerk want?" I ask after she hangs up.

Kalli opens a cupboard door, but slams it hard without looking inside. "He's not a jerk," she says, staring into the sink. "I don't care what you and Mom say, he's not."

"What did he want, Kalli?"

"It's something good. Why should I tell you?"

I yank open the fridge door. "You know what, I don't even care what he said." Through the sides of a clear plastic container, I spy furry green stuff. "What was this?" I say, tossing the entire thing into the garbage can behind me. "Kalli, remind me to buy Mom a new plastic food container-thingy."

"Dad's renting a house."

"Mom has no good food in here." I squat to open the crisper drawer.

"He lives in a place called Kincardine."

I push the drawer closed and grab a can of Diet Pepsi. "I don't know where that is and I don't care. I've got money upstairs, let's order pizza for supper."

"We get to go visit him for the whole summer."

I slam on the brakes halfway to standing. "What?"

"You heard."

I close the fridge with my foot as I spin around. "You'd better be lying."

"Nope."

"Well, I won't go," I say nonchalantly, even though my heart is threatening to kick its way out of my chest.

"Maybe you won't have a choice." Kalli smirks. "Dad said it's a custody thing."

My apathetic attitude crumbles at the word *custody*. This could be a problem.

ZZZ

"Penny, I'm at work." Sigh. "We'll talk about it when I get home."

I hold the phone away from my ear and glower at it, hoping my boiling hot anger will surge through the tiny mouthpiece holes, travel along the phone lines with the electrons, and blast out on her end. Mom's breathy, annoyed tone of voice ticks me off, but not as much as the underlying message in her response.

"You don't even sound surprised?" I squeak. "It's true, isn't it? You knew all about Dad taking us for the summer and you didn't tell me."

The dial tone buzzes in my ear.

I thought I was angry before, but no, that was a wimpy emotion compared to what I'm feeling now. I pull the receiver of the phone back past my shoulder and smash it against the base that's attached to the wall. A small chunk of plastic cracks off with an awful splintering sound and whizzes past my face, narrowly missing my eye. "Stupid, cheap piece of crap," I grumble, hanging the phone up properly.

When I turn around, the first thing I see is Kalli, gawking at me with wide eyes. She looks frightened, like she thinks she's next in line to get smacked.

"Remind me to buy Mom a new phone." I brush past her and jog into the laundry room. I can barely pull on my jacket.

The screen door clatters shut behind me. Four faded wooden steps lead up to our back door, and I leap over all of them at once, landing on the grass below. I walk. My arms whoosh back and forth, swinging like pendulums that propel me down our driveway.

In my peripheral vision, I see a car roll into view alongside the curb. It keeps pace with me as I speed down the sidewalk.

"Hey, where are you going?" a deep voice calls from inside the car.

I stop, hoping I'm not the intended fresh meat for some murderous psycho, and peer through the open passenger-side window. Ryan grins back at me.

"What are you doing here?" I ask, quickly replacing my pissed-off expression with one that's not so scary.

"I was on my way to your place to see if you want to go out for a drive, and then I saw you leave. Are you going somewhere?"

"I just needed to get out of the house for a while."

"Get in. I'll take you wherever you want to go." When I'm seated in the car, he says, "You look bummed out."

I stare at the daffodils and tulips in the flower garden beside the sidewalk. "I found out I might have to go to my dad's this summer."

"Oh. That's not a good thing?"

"I'd have to go for the whole summer."

"Oh," he says, clearly disappointed. "Want a hot fudge sundae?"

"That sounds great. Thanks." If Ryan thinks bingeing on chocolate is the best way to solve one's problems, then I'm sinking my claws into him and not letting go.

The car gets rolling down the street. I continue to stare out the window. "My parents can be such morons," I say, not really to Ryan, just out loud.

"In what way?"

I have plenty of reasons for thinking my parents are morons. But I wasn't expecting to list them. "Well, you know. Doesn't everybody think their parents are annoying?"

"Not me. My parents are awesome."

I add a helping of embarrassment to my bad mood, and look at Ryan to gauge his expression. He's staring straight ahead, eyebrows furrowed like he's concentrating on the road.

"Your parents are great." I inhale deeply. "Your dad's hilarious."

Ryan shakes his head. "I can't believe he told you that joke about the one-legged nun at dinner the other night."

I laugh, remembering the punch line. Ryan's dad has a definite raunchy streak. And he's good looking, too. For an old guy. "You look a lot like your dad."

"I know. We get that a lot," he says. "Which is weird, since I'm adopted."

Well. That came at me out of nowhere. "You are?"

"Yup."

I go back to staring out the window.

"Sorry I didn't tell you before," he says. His hand settles on my shoulder, and I jump. "I hardly ever think about it, so it's not something I remember to tell people."

"That's okay." I smile. "Do you know anything about your birth mom? Have you ever met her?"

"No way. Don't want to know who she is. Don't want to meet her."

The tension inside the car is getting thick. Luckily, the

drive-thru is upon us. As we're pulling in, Ryan and I exhale loudly. We glance at each other and start laughing. Already we're turning into one of those spooky couples who say and do things in unison.

"I don't want to meet her," Ryan says, while we're waiting in line, "but I would like to thank her somehow. If she hadn't given me up, I wouldn't have my family, the life that's perfect for me. It's like something out there, fate or whatever, searched around for my real parents and gave me to them. I lucked out." He watches his fingers tap the steering wheel. "I'm rambling. Sorry." His cheeks blush a color of red I thought only I could achieve, and he gives me an apologetic smile. "How cheesy can I get?"

I smile back, to let him know I don't mind at all that he's a cheese-ball. Looks like we both need some cheering up now.

"We should get double fudge," we say at the same time.

Downright spooky we are.

"Where were you?" Mom calls from the living room, as I close the back door.

"Out with Ryan." I slip my shoes off, preparing to make a hasty break for my room.

The couch creaks.

"I know I'm in trouble, Mom. No need to get up."

But, of course, she has to get up anyway. She'd hate to pass up an opportunity to rag on me, especially an opportunity as good as this one.

"Do you have any idea how embarrassed I was to have you

ranting on the phone while I was at work?" she says from the doorway where the kitchen and living room meet. "I had to pretend to be in a good mood in front of a huge line of customers. And my boss was standing right beside me."

Most of the time, Mom looks pretty and lots of people mistake her for my older sister. Right now, her hair is limp, her face is pale, and from head to toe she seems to be sagging, like somebody cranked up the gravity level in the house. I feel a twinge of guilt because it's probably all my fault she looks hideous.

"I'm sorry."

"And you broke the phone, for crying out loud."

"Sorry."

"And then you ran out on your sister, you didn't tell anybody where you were going, and you didn't call."

"Sorry."

"Don't be flippant with me!"

Since when is apologizing being flippant?

"Sorry." The automatic response slides out of my mouth and, unfortunately, it comes off sounding more exasperated than the others did.

Mom growls. The loud whack of her hand against the table-top jolts me to attention. "Get up to your room."

I shuffle across the kitchen, walk up a couple of stairs, and droop over the railing. "Do I really have to go to Dad's for the summer?" I ask, trying hard to tone down my anger, and failing miserably.

"You do now!"

Inside my head, I let loose a fierce barrage of swearing. I stomp upstairs.

"Stop pounding your feet like a three-year-old!"

Too bad I took my shoes off at the door. They'd come in handy now that Mom has left me no choice but to stomp down the hallway with louder and heavier steps.

A faint strip of light glows in the space beneath Kalli's bedroom door. Her mattress squeaks. "Pen, can I talk to you?"

"Make it quick."

The unicorn poster on the outside of her door flutters, and light fills the hallway.

"You're mad about going away this summer, right?"

"You could say that."

"You don't have to be mad. It'll be fun. Dad lives on a beach. And he's got a dog."

"He could have a giraffe and an elephant for all I care."

"You shouldn't be mean to Mom," she says, putting her hands on her puny hips. "She doesn't want us to go, but it's only for two months. She gets to see us for ten months. That's not very fair to Dad, is it?"

"I didn't hear anybody ask me what I thought was fair for me. I have friends. I have a job. I don't even like Dad all that much."

Kalli frowns. "You can be a real jerk sometimes."

The light fades, and when the door shuts with a soft click, I'm left fuming in the dark hallway. "I may be a lot of things. But I'm definitely not a jerk," I say, but only loud enough for the unicorn to hear.

◆◆◆ A girl who looks like me is leaning against a tree a few
feet away. If I'm over there, whose body am I watching
this dream from? It's like I stepped out from behind a video camera to film myself, but left my eyeballs behind to watch.

"Hi, Astrid," the girl says, curiously eyeing me.

I shake my head, confused. "My name is Penny."

"No, it isn't," she says, laughing. "I'm Penny."

I don't like that she's toying with me. "I am Penny. I can
feel it."

"Astrid, don't you understand? Deep inside, we are the same."
She points directly at me. "It's what's on the outside that counts."

I turn around. A full-length mirror hovers in the air in the
middle of the forest clearing. The young woman in the reflection
smiles when I smile. When I move, her dark-blond hair sways
like a combed mare's tail. I raise my hands, and she straightens
her intricately woven cloak.

Two mirrors spring up behind the first one. Behind them, four
mirrors magically appear, then six, all reflecting similar, yet different, versions of me.

The girl leaning against the tree says, "I found the key."

"The key to what?" I ask, watching her reflection in one of
the mirrors.

"My mind. I opened it and found you, Astrid. And I found
the others. I found them all."

"Open your textbooks to page one hundred and eighty . . .
blah, blah, blah."

The woman blathering away at the front of the Math

classroom is my teacher, Ms. Watford. I dislike her, not because she's bitchy, but because she's odorous. It's a scent that can only be described as wilting flowers meets old gym shoes meets death. She almost never leaves her desk, which means I have to keep a facade of rapt attention on my face at all times or she'll nail me.

I tilt my head like I'm hanging on her every mind-numbing word and think about Dad's new house. I'm beginning to wonder what it looks like. And since Dad's a pretty irresponsible guy, he might let me do stuff that Mom doesn't allow me to do. I'll go without a fight, but I'd better get my own bedroom there. That would make the trip semi-bearable. If I have to share a room with Kalli, I'll hitchhike all the way back home. Maybe. I have a slight fear of serial killers that might hinder that plan.

"Astrid."

I jerk in my desk, startled by Ms. Watford's bullfrog croak of a voice calling my name. "Yes?"

Her head turns and she scrutinizes me with squinted, beady eyes. "Does 'Aston' sound even remotely like 'Penelope'?" she asks, enunciating every syllable. "Take your head out of the clouds, please."

"I'm sorry, Ms. Watford," I stammer, but she turns her attention to Aston Miller on the other side of the room.

Great, I've just been publicly humiliated for brain doodling. The real kicker, though, is that I answered for snooty Aston Miller, who happens to be a guy. Now everybody in the class thinks I'm a spaced-out loser. And Scott sits two desks behind me. News of my idiocy will reach Ryan's ears by lunch. At least no one dares laugh at me with the Bride of the Grim Reaper standing at the front of the room.

I am the History Teacher's Pet. I wear that title proudly. I will never ever be the Math Teacher's Pet, and that's fine by me. To be Ms. Watford's pet, I'd have to be a hideous little gargoyle or something. I slump against my desk and imagine Ms. Watford melting into a giant pile of goo on the floor, trying my hardest to make it come true through telepathy. It never works. She never explodes or burns or melts.

I stare off into space with the end of my pen in my mouth. *Hmmm, we haven't had a fire drill in a really long time*, I muse, watching the hypnotic movement of the wall clock's second hand. I take the pen out of my mouth and absentmindedly fill the edges of my Math notes with stars, and circles that I turn into suns, and triangles that become sails for tiny boats.

Ms. Watford's background chatter is drowned out by the shrill buzz of an alarm. The fire alarm. I freeze in mid-doodle and stare around the room as everybody jumps up from their desks. *Wow . . . that was a weird coincidence.*

While eating my cereal this morning, I started crying. One minute I was fine, the next, I was boohooing like somebody had died. It's a good thing Kalli and Mom were engaged in a vicious battle for the bathroom at the time. And last night, I bawled like a baby over some dumb phone company commercial. As much as I want help with whatever's going on inside me, I don't want people to know I'm losing my marbles.

I'm in the middle of slipping on my shoes to go to school when the door squeaks, and Di jumps into the laundry room. "I brought you something. It's a present." She brings a spiral-bound book out from behind her back and holds it out for me to take. "You can use it at your dad's."

I take the book and study the cover art. The beach scene in the background, clear blue water and a rocky cliff, looks normal. On the shore, melting clocks hang limp from a tree branch and a wooden box and the melting profile of a face. A closed pocket watch on the wooden box is covered in big black ants.

"It's a dream journal," she says, practically bouncing in place.

Oh no. Di got me a journal to write my crazy dreams in.

"You don't like it, Pen? I got the idea from Val."

"No, I love it. I'm trying to figure out the cover, that's all."

"It's a picture of a Salvador Dali painting called *Persistence of Memory*. When I saw the book, I knew it would be the perfect dream journal."

Persistence of Memory. A shudder twitches through my shoulders and into my face.

"It's surreal. Just like a dream," I say.

Di laughs. "Well, it should be. Dali was a Surrealist."

I don't know what a Surrealist is, but Di's brain absorbs art history like mine absorbs useless trivia. "Thanks, Di." I stick the journal inside my backpack. "I'll start using it today. I promise."

Dear Dream Journal:

For the first time in recorded history, Ms. Watford left her desk just now. The class is shocked. Rumors of her possible whereabouts are flying. My guess is she hobbled back to the grave.

I've decided to use this book to write about my dreams after all. Maybe if I get them down on paper, they'll leave my head, and I won't think about them so much.

Marie Antoinette:

1) Diana was my best friend. She was killed by an angry mob and her head was paraded past Marie Antoinette's jail window.

2) Hans was my lover. In the dream, he was wearing

a lion mask, and he set a red rose on the bed. He was ripped to pieces by an angry mob, too.

I also had a dream that I was a girl named Astrid. Please, please, please, let that be the only one, and not the beginning of a bunch more wacko lucid dreams.

I'm curled up on the couch in the living room, in the dark, watching TV with the volume off. Until eleven I watched TV with Di, Scott, and Ryan. Then they deserted me, citing some lame reason like they have to get up early for school. It didn't help that Mom walked into the living room and said, "It's time for everybody to go home now."

It must be nearly two o'clock, but with sleep come dreams, so I'm putting off going to bed for as long as I can. There's no way for me to know if my dreams will be the normal kind where I show up for an exam naked, or more of the psychotic kind where my best friend is bloody or dead. I haven't felt this nervous about bedtime since second grade, when I wore turtlenecks under my nightgowns to prevent vampire attacks. I was weird then, and I'm still weird.

As soon as this TV show is finished, I'll go up to bed. I will. For sure. Unless, of course, another good show comes on. But I'll definitely go to bed after that one.

Beams of moonlight filter into the forest, silhouetting the evergreens. The birch trees cast an eerie white glow.

Sensing a presence next to me, I turn my head. There, nearly melding with the darkness, is a large raven. It coasts through the air, wings spread wide, regarding me with curious brown eyes that glisten like marbles.

"Run faster, Astrid," the raven says, in the voice of a young girl.

"I can't," I cry, frustrated. "I can't run any faster."

The raven's wings beat hard. "You must. Time is short. Hurry."

I force my heavy legs to move. The raven effortlessly soars off down the path, and I send an envious cry after it.

"I can't do this!" I shout into the darkness.

The raven's firm voice reverberates through the forest. "You can."

I stumble out of the trees into a starlit clearing—in time to see Diana and a young man step to the edge of a rocky cliff that juts out over the tumultuous sea far below. He drops a red rose and takes Di's hand. This can't be happening. I need to shout to them, but no words will come out. Their beautiful cloaks glide out behind them as they leap into the air. And they plummet out of sight.

In my ear, the raven whispers, "You were too late."

Dear Dream Journal:

I had another bad dream last night. Di and the millennium guy I dreamed about before jumped off a cliff into the ocean. I didn't get there in time to stop them. If I had just run faster, and gotten there seconds sooner, could I have saved them?

 Summer vacation is mere
seconds away. I'm the only person in the room, probably in the
whole school, paralyzed by depression. If my parents loved me
as much as they claim to, they'd let me stay home with my
friends and my new boyfriend this summer.

The bell rings, and excited cheers fill the classroom. I gather up my stuff and struggle to standing. When I get to my locker, which seems to take forever, I take a seat on the floor in front of it, not caring if I get trampled. I rest my face on my knees.

A large hand rubs my back.

"Hi, Ryan," I murmur.

"What's wrong?" he whispers in my ear, and his breath tickles my skin.

"My life sucks," I want to wail, but instead I say, "Nothing."

"The party at Trevor's tonight will be huge." He tucks my hair behind my ear. "We'll have enough fun to hold you over until you get back from your dad's. Okay?"

I slowly lift my head, feeling totally bogged down. "Okay."

"My parents went away to the cottage last night," he says in my ear.

I smile, but it's probably not even visible.

Ryan stands and puts out a hand to help me up from the floor. Right in front of a ton of other people, he leans over and gives me a long kiss. His lips seem to absorb my sadness. When he pulls away, I'm so tingly I'll probably electrocute the next person who touches me.

If I get much more drunk, I'll be pickle-ized or something. I know the smile on my face is stupid, but I can't get rid of it. It only goes away when I take a slurp of beer. Well, I guess it goes away pretty often then.

"Hi, gorgeous."

My head moves in slow motion. Ryan takes a seat on the couch beside me.

"Hi yourself." My lips do a weird sputtery thing. "You think *I'm* gorgeous? You're crazy. You know who's really gorgeous? Diana, that's who. She's been my best friend for, like, the past zillion years," I say, staring into his beautiful green eyes. "And you know what? Every time she's been my best friend, she's died." I pause, methodically rubbing the bottom of his shirt. "And I always feel guilty, you know? Like it's my fault. Like I'm not taking good enough care of her. Do you get what I'm saying?"

"Mmmm, no." Ryan points toward the keg. "Diana's right there. Why don't you go over and talk to her?"

Di's body is firmly pressed against Scott's, which is risky because his vengeful ex-girlfriend, Leslie, is at this party. And she's been giving Di a hard time lately.

Leslie's leaning against the wall near the stereo, holding two full drinks. Guess she's trying to get blasted two times faster than normal. Her friend Marissa looks on, with her typical sarcastic scowl, as Leslie yaps nonstop like a little poodle. I hate poodles. They are so kickable.

I step over the legs of people seated on the floor, as gracefully as a herd of elephants barreling over to a water hole. "Di, I love you more than anyone."

"I love you, too." She uncaps her flavored water and takes a sip.

"You know what?" I say, swaying to and fro like I'm standing in a canoe. "If Leslie thinks she can get away with hurting my best friend, I say *screw her*!"

This statement sends a deer-in-headlights expression shooting across Scott's face.

Di laughs and gives me a one-armed hug. "Good for you, Pen. Go kick her ass."

The room is packed with people. I make my way over to Leslie, and leer at her.

She chugs one of her drinks and sets the glass on a speaker. "What's your problem?"

"You've been harassing my friend Diana," I say, putting on my evilest face.

"What of it?"

"You're going to stop. Are you understanding me?"

"Listen," she says, scowling. "Tell your whore friend to stay away from Scott." She gives me a shove, and I hear her say, "Ryan is way too good for you, you cow."

The room whirls around me. I stumble backward and bump into Ryan.

"What's going on here?" he asks.

"She just shoved me and called me a cow."

Leslie's mouth drops open and her face goes red in an instant. "I did not!" she cries. "But, hey, if the udder fits . . ."

I try to lunge forward, but Ryan pulls me back.

"Shut up, Leslie. I mean it." He leads me to the arm of the couch, where I take a seat. "Pen, I came up behind you before Les shoved you. I didn't hear her call you a cow."

In his eyes, I can see that he wants to believe me, but he didn't hear her say it.

Totally confused, I say, "No, she did. I heard her."

But did I hear her words with my ears or inside my head?, I wonder, thinking back on our encounter. Am I hearing voices now? Is that what's going on? Several people are gawking in my direction. A giant wave of embarrassment crashes over me.

"What happened?" Di hollers, arriving out of nowhere. "Did she hit you?"

I take a deep breath, eager to talk about something else. "She didn't hit me."

We glance at the other side of the room, where Leslie is chatting it up with half the football team, probably telling them what a spastic freak the cow on the couch is.

"What do you say we head over to my place now?" Ryan says.

Di pulls me to standing. "Good idea."

ᴢᴢᴢ

"It's late, Pen. I should go home."

I tilt my head back on my lawn chair and look at Di upside down. "Already?"

"I don't want to get run-down. Rehearsal's coming up."

I walk with Di to the side of Ryan's house. At the end of the driveway, Scott is patiently waiting to walk her home.

"What am I supposed to do for the next two months?" Di says. "Tell your dad he can take Kalli, but you have to stay here."

I wish she'd quit looking at me like I'm abandoning her. I feel bad enough about having to leave.

"Trust me, I'd stay if I could. But it's not up to me."

"But who's going to eat my M&M's after I pick the brown ones out for myself? Who's going to braid your hair when it's really hot out? You know hair isn't your thing. You'll be all sweaty and stringy."

"Thank you."

Di tugs on her long, fringed bangs, like she does when she's upset. "E-mail and instant message me every day. Does your dad have a webcam?"

"I doubt it. Since he doesn't even have a computer."

"What?" Di cries, probably waking half the neighbors. "Is he prehistoric? Does he expect you to chisel messages into rocks? How am I supposed to talk to you for free?"

My plan was to make a lot of long-distance phone calls. I assumed Dad would be okay with that. He goes almost a whole year without needing to spend money on us. Now that I think about it, maybe I should come up with a more feasible plan.

"There must be a library where my dad lives. I'll e-mail you from there when I can."

Di gives me a hug. "You'd better. If I stop e-mailing back, I've died of boredom."

At the end of the driveway, Scott straightens from his laid-back slouch and takes a few backward steps to the sidewalk. "Coming, Di?"

In my ear, Di says, "Thanks for sticking up for me tonight over the Leslie thing. If you ever need me to, I'll do the same for you. In a heartbeat."

Our hug ends. And our summer apart begins.

I watch Di bound down the driveway, so lightly I almost expect her to lift off and fly.

"Talk to you soon," she says, as Scott puts his arms around her waist.

I just wave good-bye. I don't feel very good all of a sudden.

I locate Ryan's dark shape in the backyard and head in that direction. My lawn chair squeaks beneath me. I tilt my head back and stare at the sky. A shooting star streaks over us, and I quickly wish I'd never talked to Margie.

"Did you know koalas almost never drink?" Ryan says.

If that's his attempt to cheer me up, it's working. "That's a relief. If they got drunk, they'd fall out of their trees."

He laughs. "They get their water from the eucalyptus leaves they eat."

Now it's my turn to tell Ryan a fun-fact. It's a game we made up while driving home from his swim meet last week.

"Did you know that dolphins swim in circles when they sleep? They keep the one eye on the outside of the circle open to watch for sharks."

"Cool. Did you know that barber poles are red and white because barbers used to do medical stuff like bleed people? They hung the blood-stained rags out to dry on a pole."

"Interesting," I say. "Did you know that the Mona Lisa has no eyebrows?"

"No, I didn't."

"Di told me that."

We go back to staring at the sky for a while.

"There's the Big Dipper." The starry scoop is obvious, but I point to it anyway.

"The Big Dipper is part of a constellation called Ursa Major. And the Little Dipper's in Ursa Minor. The star at the end of its handle is Polaris, the North Star."

"Show off," I tease.

I glance at his silhouette in the dark. I don't need to see him to know he's blushing. He has no problem walking around in a bathing suit that leaves little to the imagination, but he can't take a compliment or joke without lighting up like a Christmas tree.

"I like astronomy," he says. "Anything that has to do with ancient civilizations, I love. Greeks, Egyptians, Incas. I can't get enough of it."

This is definitely not the time to confess that I enrolled in History solely to gaze upon Mr. Lamont's gorgeous face and behind.

Ryan reaches into the front pouch of his sweatshirt and pulls out a CD case. "Pen, I burned this CD for you. It's a bunch of songs I thought you'd like. I made myself a copy, too. That way we can listen at the same time and it'll be kind of like we're together."

My shaking hand reaches out to take the case. I wasn't expecting Ryan to give me anything and this CD seems like way too much. The only good-bye gift I'm giving him is the pleasure of spending the evening in my half-tanked presence. *Whoopdeedoo.*

"Thanks," I say, unable to say anything more than that.

"The Queen songs are from the movie *The Highlander.* Have you seen it?"

"No. Maybe we can see it when I get home."

I rest my head on his shoulder and bury my face against his neck. His scent fills my nose, firing up nerve endings that tell my inebriated brain to jump his bones. It's scary, but the words *I love you* are clicking against the back of my teeth. I want to open my mouth and let them loose. But something's holding me back.

When I imagine myself saying those words to Ryan, I feel guilty. As if I've already promised to say them to someone else.

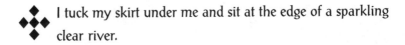 I tuck my skirt under me and sit at the edge of a sparkling clear river.

"Astrid, there you are!"

I twist to look behind me. Diana throws her waist-length golden braid over her shoulder with a mischievous smile.

"She's here, Raven! At the water!" Di calls out as she runs to the river's edge.

A statuesque girl strides out from the evergreens, extraordinary black hair streaming out behind her. In a strange tongue, my own shocked voice fills my mind, saying, "Hrefna!" Raven.

"We were watching Leif and Erik wrestle," Di sighs. Her flowing dress billows when she plunks down next to me.

Just as Raven stretches out on the grass, the ground rumbles, and a group of boys, stripped to their breeches, thunders into the river. A leather boot sails through the air, narrowly missing my head, and tumbles onto the soggy riverbank.

"Come for a swim, Raven Thunder-Trousers!" a cute boy with a hint of blond scruff on his face taunts, waist-deep in swirling water.

Raven leaps to her feet and storms fully clothed into the river.

Diana and I laugh when she tackles the boy. They exchange a few words, and her fist snaps out to slug him in the stomach. He keels into the water, smirking. Wading to the river's edge, she angrily wrings out her hair. But the dreamy look in her eyes tells a different story.

I grab a fine-tooth bone comb from my skirt and run it through Raven's wet hair until it shines blue-black in the sunshine.

"Leif can't take his eyes off you." She shifts to look at me, and the comb slides out of her hair. "What did you do? Cast a spell over him?"

Within the group of blond- and copper-haired boys splashing in the river, only one stands out—the handsome young man watching me comb Raven's hair. All the others have blended together, as if to form one man I don't need to pay attention to. I feel drawn to Leif.

Raven grabs my hand, stopping it in a mid-air sweep, and I snap free of my daze. "Did you talk to your father about Erik?" she asks. "My brother would make a wonderful husband, Astrid. He asks about you all the time. And if you marry him, we'll be sisters."

I sit tall, excited and proud that both Leif and Erik want me. How far would they go to win my heart?

"Today at the distance-swimming competition," I begin slowly, "they will swim as far as they can into the open sea. Whoever turns back last will become my husband. I will leave the decision up to them."

On the other side of me, Diana gasps. "You can't do that. Your family will choose your husband." Close to tears, she adds, "And Raven's right. Erik would be a wonderful, caring husband. You don't need to marry Leif to be happy."

I pull my arm free from Raven's tightening grasp. "My parents are divorced. My father will listen to my wishes and do what I want him to do." Crossing my arms, I go back to gaping at Leif. "Whoever loves me more will win."

Dear Dream Journal:
I had another dream about Astrid. Di and Raven met me at a river, after watching Leif and Erik wrestle.

Leif was the millennium guy. Everything about him seemed so exciting, like brand-new love. Was he the first, a thousand years ago?

As I was waking up, Ryan ran in front of Leif, and asked me if I wanted to watch a movie. That made me mad because he was blocking my view of Leif, and I knew I only had seconds of dreamtime left. My subconscious must be trying to remind me that I have a real, live boyfriend who I should be dreaming about. Instead, I'm fantasizing about another guy. Once I figured that out, I felt awful. Am I making Ryan compete with someone who exists only in my dreams??

"Your father's going to be here any minute. I think I'm going to throw up."

"Yeah, me too," I mutter, and Mom scowls as she paces past me. I believe she has correctly guessed I have a hangover.

"Dad's here!" Kalli hollers from upstairs.

"Oh, shit," Mom and I say at the same time. We laugh about it, but then Mom's face tenses up in a flash. "Watch your mouth," she says.

Kalli thumps downstairs and struggles to get through the kitchen doorway, lugging her suitcases and bags.

"Did you pack your whole room, or what?"

She lets everything fall to the floor. "We're going for the whole summer. *Duh.*"

The doorbell rings. Kalli squeals and runs to the front door, waving her arms in the air like an idiot. Dad knows we use the back door. Why'd he ring at the front? Maybe he feels like a stranger at our house now.

"I want him out of here. Get moving," Mom says, stepping around Kalli's junk.

"Geez, fine."

"Hello, Karen," Dad calls into the house, and I unexpectedly smile. The sound of his voice chisels away the ice coating that was preserving the four-year-old girl I used to be, the girl who loved her dad unconditionally and thought he was the coolest guy around.

"Hello, Peter," Mom says, stiffer than a wooden spoon. She hurries into the main-floor bathroom and shuts the door.

I set the crust of my buttered toast on my plate. "Hi, Dad."

"Penny!"

Kalli gallops into the kitchen from the living room, with Dad not far behind. He looks really uncomfortable, like his skin is itching to leap off his skeleton and sprint away. The smile he gives me has a hint of surprise in it. I wonder if I look different from the last time he saw me almost a year ago. I'm stunned by Dad's appearance. He must have quit drinking, because he's lost at least thirty pounds.

I have none of Dad's genes in me, and I'll hate to the day I die that Kalli got his height and I didn't. That dummy will no doubt be a supermodel within ten years, sleeping with rock stars, living the good life, and traveling the world, while I'll be married to a two-timing loser, popping out kids, and squashing the wide hips I got from Mom's side of the family onto the worn-out cat-clawed sofa to eat ice cream straight from the carton while watching soap operas.

"All set?" Dad asks.

My bag is lying on the kitchen floor, looking puny next to Kalli's mountain of luggage. I slept late and packed at the last minute. Unless Dad lives north of the Arctic Circle, there's sure to be a mall in his town. I can buy whatever I forgot.

I loop the straps of my bag over my shoulder. "I guess."

Dad clears his throat. "Say good-bye to your mother. I'll meet you out at the car."

"Mom, we're leaving!" Kalli shouts.

The front door closes. Mom leaves the bathroom, patting her face with toilet paper.

"Mom, don't cry. Just think of all the fun you can have without Kalli and me here."

Mom whimpers behind the toilet paper.

Kalli runs over and gives her a quick peck on the cheek.

Mom holds her arms out. I set my bag on the floor, shuffle over, and allow her to squeeze me. I keep my arms at my sides, feeling even less affectionate than usual.

"See you in a couple of months," I say, as she crushes air from my lungs.

"You be careful."

"I will, Mom. I'll call when we get there." I wiggle out of her clutches and grab my bag. "I should go. Dad's waiting."

Mom follows me to the back door, where I grab my jacket and put on my shoes. Mom follows me through the living room to the front door. Mom follows me out the door.

Dad's car, a very brand-new-looking Honda Accord, is idling in the driveway. We never had new, shiny black cars with leather interiors while Dad was with us. We were lucky if they came equipped with working seat belts.

"Nice car," Mom says. A person lacking people-reading skills would take that as a compliment. But I heard venom drip from her fangs to the asphalt and, *"Nice car where'd you get the money for that you never had money to spend on us."*

I set my bag in the open trunk, on top of Kalli's layer of luggage. Kalli took the front passenger seat, so I get the whole backseat to myself.

Within seconds, we're rolling down my street. The street I've lived on my whole life. I turn to glance out the rear window, and see Mom waving her arm through the air. I give a small good-bye wave and turn back around in my seat, already missing Di and Ryan.

Up front, Dad and Kalli chat nonstop. I'm only half listening, but then Kalli turns in her seat, giving me a smirk. "Penny's got a boyfriend now."

Brat.

Dad glances into the rearview mirror to look at me. "The same boy-hating Penny who declared at the age of ten that she'd never, ever have a boyfriend or get married?"

"Yup, that same Penny. I think boys are only mildly vile and nauseating now."

Dad asks me a few innocent questions about Ryan, and I give a few succinct answers that don't reveal too much.

Kalli, probably ticked off that the conversation isn't revolving around her, starts giving Dad a minute-by-minute replay of the past year. I silently pray for a bus to hit us. If I go to sleep, maybe I'll be oblivious to the long car ride and Kalli's lame stories.

I slouch down and gently rest my head against the back of the seat. Through my eyelashes, I watch grassy hills and clumps of forest whiz past my window—

❖❖❖ My head bobs sleepily and I fix my gaze on Margie, who's sharing the backseat with me. Her grin exposes a smudge of pink lipstick on her front teeth.

Framing the window with her hands, she says, "I told you you'd be traveling."

"Lucky guess." I watch the scenery roll past my own window.

"Like I said, Penny, everything happens for a reason."

"Do I have to go to Dad's for a reason?" I turn to look at her. "I'm not going to meet that thousand-year-old guy there, am I? The guy from my dreams?"

Margie shrugs, and as I'm staring at her, I notice that the car we're riding in isn't my dad's car. The whole shape is different, boxy, not sleek and rounded. And everything is worn, not new. The seat is gray and fuzzy, and there's a tiny cigarette burn in the fabric, beside my right leg. Who does this car belong to?

"It's a shame you had to leave Diana," Margie says with a wistful sigh.

Up goes my head again. "What do you mean?"

The red curls on the back of Margie's head slither and intertwine in a slow, hypnotic dance. "It's for the best," she says, staring out the window. A coil of hair rears up and strikes out at me, sprouting black eyes and curved fangs an inch from my face. My head flies back and crunches against the window glass.

In unison, the snake-like curls jut upward, like a venomous forest. A horrific wail fills the car. My hands fly to my ears to block it out, but it's no good. It's not only coming from the mouths of the snakes, it's inside my head, too. With a **whoosh**, the snakes burst into flame. Fire flashes across the roof of the car in a rolling wave, rippling down Margie's seat belt.

Pressing my body against my door, I say, "Tell me. Why did I have to leave!"

The fire-engulfed head turns away from the blackened window. But the mangled face staring back at me from the fire isn't Margie's, it's Diana's. Rotting hunks of white flesh flap off her cheeks, the skin on her forehead bubbles angrily, licked by flames. Worms of blue fire weave through her lips.

I claw at the gray plastic in search of a door handle, terrified.

"Pen, you had to leave," Diana whispers, and she leans so close I can see the reflection of the flames in her eyes, "to get away from me."

"*Whaaaaaa,* " I blurt, wrenching awake.

The car lurches as if Dad, startled, tapped the brakes as a reflex.

"Everything all right back there?" he asks.

Breathe, breathe, breathe. "Yeah, Dad." A vibration of fear hums through me.

"Don't tell me you had another stupid dream," Kalli says. I can't see her eyes, but I know they're rolling back. Maybe one of these times, they'll snap and stay that way.

I stare at a lackadaisical herd of cows in the field outside my window, not wanting to talk about the fire-car dream. But then I start to wonder why Kalli kind of implied that stupid dreams are the norm for me.

"What do you mean, Kalli?"

More unseen eye rolling. "You wake me up almost every night with your moaning and whimpering and saying dumb stuff like 'Malcolm, don't leave me,' or 'don't die, Raphael.' Every time I get up to go pee in the night, I hear you."

No way. She must be lying. I suddenly feel sick, like somebody told me I compulsively pick my nose in public without being aware of it. If Kalli is telling the truth, and I do have weird dreams way more often than I thought . . . what on earth am I dreaming about? And who the heck are Malcolm and Raphael?

After a few hours of nothing but cows, sheep, flat fields, and the occasional nearly nonexistent town outside my window, I start to get nervous. If Dad lives in some hole-in-the-ground town full of rednecks and old people, I'm going to die.

"We're almost there," Dad announces as we pass, heaven help me, a cheese factory.

I've entered the Land of Cattle and Cheese.

We pull off the highway. The town itself seems pretty normal. The houses are cute, the lawns are green, and the gardens are full of flowers. We cruise past a grocery store and a community center. So far, I haven't seen a single teenager. Even the playground is empty. And the car ahead of us is crawling down the street as if doing the speed limit is a sin punishable by death. The *Twilight Zone* theme goes off in my head. This really is an old-person town, I just know it.

"Why did you move here?" I ask.

"He works at an automotive plant," Kalli says. "Mom said he makes lots of money."

Dad chuckles.

"Wow, there are lots of big trees here," Kalli, the master of astute observation, says.

Dad points to a building that's so old the bricks are crumbling. "There's the theater. You girls might like the movie that's playing there now, it's a teen movie."

The movie? As in singular?

"I can see the beach!" Kalli cries, like she's never seen a flippin' lake before.

While we're stopped at the intersection beside the theater, which, according to Dad, is smack-dab in the middle of downtown, Kalli and I get a quick rundown of good places to eat, shop, and hang out. The buildings downtown all look as old as the theater and there are no recognizable fast food signs visible. A mall has yet to make an appearance.

"This is a big tourist town," Dad says. "It's really hopping in the summer."

Apparently.

The light turns green and we continue on toward the lake. The patch of turquoise and navy blue water in the distance gets bigger. The street dips into a steep hill that ends at the beach, and I nearly shout out an ecstatic "woo hoo!" No wonder the town felt slow as we drove through. All the young people are at the beach.

Kalli starts chattering away about ten different things at once, but I stare out my window, mesmerized by how pictur-esque the scenery is.

"My house isn't far from here," Dad says, and the beach disappears from sight. We drive for a few minutes, and then the lake pops back into view. The car slows. Gravel crunches beneath the tires. "Here we are."

Inside my head, I can't help but chant a flabbergasted cho-rus of *Dad lives on the beach . . . Dad lives on the beach.* I fumble for the door handle. Hot air blasts my face when I open the door.

"It's not a large cottage, but it's winterized for year-round use," Dad says, almost apologetically, while shutting off the car.

The front passenger door slams. Kalli sprints across the lawn, heading for a tree-lined path beside the cottage that leads down to the beach. "It's awesome, Dad!"

I have to agree. Dad's house isn't very big, like he said, but it's got a windowed sunroom and a huge wraparound deck. And it barks.

"There's someone who wants to meet you." Dad strides across the lawn and jogs up the deck steps. Before he's got the door open all the way, a mass of golden fur comes exploding out. "Sandy, sit, girl," Dad says from the deck.

The furry bullet skids to a stop, obediently parking her butt on the ground in front of me. Golden brown eyes gaze up at me with adoration, and Sandy gives me a lolling-tongue doggie smile to say she's already claimed me as a friend.

Dad has a golden retriever . . . Dad has a golden retriever!

Dad rushes over, panting even more than the dog. "Sandy's still a puppy and she gets a little excited."

"That's okay," I say, rubbing the silky shag of fur behind her ears. "She's so cute."

"She's cute all right, and she knows it."

Sandy cocks her head, glancing back and forth between us as if to say, "Enough of the chitchat, when is somebody gonna play with me?"

"There's something else I want to show you," Dad says.

I follow him to a rundown shed at the edge of the lawn, wondering what he wants to show me. He grabs the handles of the large wooden doors and pulls them open, revealing a car. I stare at it with big question marks floating around above my head. Finally, the little lightbulb goes on.

"No way," I say, shaking my head in disbelief.

"Yes way."

If this car is Dad's way of buying my affection, then I am so bought.

"It's nothing special, but it should get you and Kalli from point A to point B," he says in the same apologetic voice he used to describe the cottage. "You'll probably spend most of your time at the beach, but I thought you should have a car around while I'm at work, just in case. And, well, it will give you some freedom while you're here."

I can't talk. I can't move. This isn't like Dad at all. Dad's not generous. Dad doesn't think of other people's needs.

"I don't know what to say."

He chuckles. "How about thanks?"

I feel a little embarrassed for not coming up with the thanks thing myself, but make up for it by giving him a quick hug. "Thanks so much, Dad."

"You're welcome. Now go check it out, the keys are already in it."

My feet decide that checking out the car would be a pretty cool thing to do. In a flash, I'm sitting in the driver's seat with both hands on the wheel. My gaze scans around in crazy circles, not focusing on anything for very long. I know I should be locating the lights and all the other necessary switches and knobs, but my brain is doing double Dutch. *Wheeeee-hoooooo!*

It's about a thousand degrees in the car because it's summer and the windows are rolled up. With a delirious smile on my face, I take one last look around. My smile sags.

The interior of the car is oddly familiar. It's old, boxy, and well worn from decades of use. Reluctantly, I turn around to check out the backseat. And my enthusiasm evaporates into the stifling air. On the seat, next to the back door, is a small, round cigarette burn.

8

"So you have lots of bad dreams?" Dad asks, as we're sitting on the deck, scarfing down the delicious chicken he barbecued for dinner.

I shrug while licking sauce off my fingers. I'm still freaked out about the car from my dream coincidence; I'm not about to give Dad the lowdown on my nightmares.

"You had bad dreams all the time when you were little," he says. "Like clockwork, around three in the morning, we'd hear you calling for Mom because you'd had another bad dream, and she'd stagger off to your bed. You always had such an imagination, Penny. It never shut off, even when you were asleep."

What kind of husband lets his wife go without sleep for years and then reminisces about it in a fond, remember-the-good-old-days kind of way? That's going to cost Dad two of the brownie points he scored today.

"And I'll never forget when you were seven or eight"—he reaches for a napkin and rubs his mouth—"you'd tell me you knew exactly what was going to happen every day because you'd dreamed it the night before. You were just the smartest little—"

Kalli's chair scrapes across the deck, cutting Dad off. "Can I go down to the beach?"

"Yeah, I guess, but don't go too far."

Staring at a wispy cloud, I mull over what Dad just told me and a fuzzy memory pops out of storage in my brain. I'm sitting on the floor in front of our Christmas tree, surrounded by mounds of discarded wrapping paper. "I knew it! I knew it!" I'm shouting. "Remember, I always dream what's going to happen the next day, and last night I had a dream that Santa got me skates. I knew he would and he did." I can't see Dad in the memory, but from above me, he says, "Yeah, that used to happen to me when I was a kid," just like that, all nonchalant, like neither of us had said anything weird.

"Oh, there's the phone." Dad pushes his chair back from the patio table and runs into the kitchen through the sliding screen door.

I trail my spoon through the mound of potato salad on my plate, feeling disconnected from reality, from everything that's going on around me, like Dad's in the kitchen and Kalli's at the beach and I'm in outer space. I hate when my real life feels like a dream. I spend way too much time dreaming as it is.

My first Saturday night at Dad's. This should be interesting. What does everybody do on a Saturday night in this dinky town? Perhaps there's a bingo game scheduled or a lawn-bowling tournament or a contest to see whose dentures fit the snuggest.

I've spent the last couple of hours collecting pretty rocks

on the beach with Kalli, and throwing pieces of driftwood into the lake for Sandy to run and swim after, a game she'd gladly play all night, I swear.

I find an amazing pink rock near the shore and add it to my collection. Dad calls to us from the cottage. Kalli and I, both on our hands and knees on the sand, gather up our rock collections, using the T-shirts we're wearing over our bathing suits as baskets. With Sandy cavorting alongside me, I race past Kalli, through the tree-lined path that leads to the cottage, and up the deck steps.

"Sandy drooled on my leg again!" Kalli shrieks, as if the dog spit acid at her. "Ewww!"

I unfold the saggy bottom of my shirt and let my stones tumble onto the patio table.

Kalli runs up behind me, out of breath. "What did you want, Dad?"

Dad, looking freshly showered, walks out to the deck from the kitchen holding Sandy's leash. "You girls change your clothes. We're going to the Pipe Band Parade."

"The Pipe what?" I ask. I'd bet good money this is an old-person thing. And judging by Dad's slickified appearance, it's a hotbed of available middle-aged women.

"You know what bagpipes are," he says. "This town has a Scottish heritage and during the summer, the Pipe Band marches every Saturday night."

This is sounding . . . unusual. Kalli and I exchange nervous glances.

"I'll go, Dad," Kalli says, pulling a bathing suit wedgie out of her butt.

I'm not sure I want to spend the evening with Dad at this Pipe thing. Kalli kicks me in the shin. "All right, I'll go," I say, narrowing my eyes at her.

By eight o'clock, we're cleaned up and on our way downtown, with Sandy leading the way. She doesn't heel for Dad when he walks her, and every so often, she lets out a *yaaak* cough because she's straining against her collar.

When we get to the traffic lights downtown, I'm shocked by how many people are already here. The sidewalks on both sides of the street are jam-packed. People are sitting on chairs, benches, and the curbs, or standing on the sidewalks talking.

"Do you want to get ice cream before the band starts?" Dad asks.

Kalli and I giddily shout, "Yes!" like we're five-year-olds, and we walk down the street to the ice cream parlor. The three employees crammed inside the tiny building bump into each other repeatedly as they hurriedly make cones for the long line. It's kind of funny to watch.

Dad pulls a ten from his wallet and holds it out for me to take. "You and Kalli get your cones. Sandy and I will go wait at the bench over there."

I glance behind him to check out the position of the bench and snatch the money from his hand. "Thanks, Dad. You're great," I say in a Scottish accent. I like talking like that. The words seem to roll right out of my mouth.

Kalli and I go to the back of the line, trying to come to an agreement on which flavors we want. By the time we're next in line, we've changed our minds about fifty times each. There are way too many delicious ice cream flavors on the planet.

"I dare you to order in Scottish," Kalli whispers in my ear with a giggle.

"What'll you give me if I do?"

"A quarter."

I cackle, startling the lady in front of me. "C'mon, Kalli, make it worth my while."

Her eyes roll back exaggeratedly. "Fine. Two dollars."

Two bucks. Well, it's not a lot, but it will get me fries at the beach tomorrow.

"You're on," I tell her, as we step up to the parlor window.

The lady behind the counter pushes her glasses up with the back of her hand, smiling at me. "What can I get you?"

Here goes. "I'll have one scoop Rocky Road and one scoop Chocolate Chip Cookie Dough," I say in a warbling Scottish accent. Kalli pokes me in the back, and I place her order, too, again in a Scottish accent. How mortifying. To hell with eating my ice cream, I'm going to apply it to my flaming red cheeks.

"Are you here visiting for the summer?" the ice cream lady asks, and I nod. "I have relatives in Scotland," she says, handing me my cone. "Whereabouts are you from?"

Yikes! "I'm from Aberdeen, it's in the northern part of Scotland," I blurt. Is that a real town in Scotland? Not sure where that answer came from, but at least I said something.

"We have a sheep farm," I say, unable to turn off my Scottish mouth. Help.

While scooping Kalli's cone, the ice cream lady smiles and says, "I'm not familiar with Aberdeen. I hope you have a wonderful holiday and enjoy the parade."

I thank her, pay for the cones, get my change, and speed away.

"We have a sheep farm?" Kalli says when she meets me at the bench. "I dared you to order in a Scottish accent, not lie and make up a big dumb story."

"I didn't mean to say that stuff, it just came out. I was nervous."

Dad stares at us from the bench like we're both crazy.

"Now you can't get ice cream from there again unless you pretend to be Scottish."

"You dared me to do it!"

"Are you two ready?" Dad says, but he's drowned out by the wail of what sounds like a dozen geese being fed into a wood chipper in the parking lot behind us.

With a melting glob of ice cream in her mouth, Kalli cries, "They're starting!"

We find a place to stand farther down the sidewalk, between two sets of elderly couples on lawn chairs. Sandy sits patiently beside me, despite the noise and the crowd, and tolerates a few pats on the head from strangers hurrying past.

The band is playing music now, music that's growing louder. I crane my neck, wanting to chant, "They're coming.

They're coming." But I'd never do something like that. I step off the curb to get a better look. They are coming, marching straight and tall, each piper and drummer wearing a uniform complete with a kilt and white knee socks. The leader of the band is holding this wickedly long silver staff thing. And the drumbeats are rollicking and upbeat, not what I'd expected to hear from a pipe band. It's a pipe band song, but with a touch of rock music snuck in. It's distinct. It's . . . cool.

I turn around to smile at Dad, and Kalli snickers at me from behind her ice cream cone. "You were dancing."

"I was not," I protest.

"Were too."

So maybe I was tapping my foot. And sashaying my hips a little. It's not like I was break-dancing or doing a striptease right out on the main street. Ignoring Kalli, I turn around to catch the end of the band as they march away with a large crowd following behind. I must admit, I'm having a great time. I was so captivated as they marched past that I neglected my ice cream. Gooey trails are dripping down my hand.

Dear Dream Journal:
I'm sitting on my top bunk (didn't get my own room—sharing one with Kalli and we have bunk beds—grrrrrr), staring out the window at my incredible view of the lake. Finally remembered a dream about that Malcolm guy. He was ruggedly handsome with reddish-brown hair and he was wearing a kilt, but I think my

brain added that in because I went to the Pipe Band.

Kalli and I found this place down at the beach that has the most amazing fries. We'll probably go there every day for the rest of the summer, so I'm going to start taking Sandy for walks. This is my plan—go for a morning walk on the beach, eat fries at the beach, and then lie on the beach all day while Dad's at work. It's a tough life, but somebody's gotta do it.

"Hi! How's everything going at your dad's?"

I smile, thrilled to hear Di's voice again. "Gee, you're home for once."

I've called her five times since I got to Dad's, but she was never there. According to her mom, Di "hit it off beautifully with the kids next door and hasn't been home much." Whatever. As far as I knew, their neighbor was a mummified old lady.

"I'm home for a couple minutes. Then I'm going to Rick and Emma's."

"Rick and Emma?"

"You'll never believe this. Mrs. Peterson went to an old folks' home."

"Shocking. And she was only, what, a hundred and eighty?"

"Pen, a seventeen-year-old stud moved into her house."

"Seriously?"

"Rick's dad just took a teaching job at our high school. That's why they moved in next door to *meeeee*!" Di sucks in a breath. "Who have you been hanging out with at your dad's?"

"Sandy. She's a dog."

Silence. "Oh. Well, that's probably fun, right?"

"Yeah, it is."

To get off my friendship with a dog, I tell Di about my car. That gets a huge reaction from her. I don't mention that I haven't actually driven it farther than the supermarket a couple of blocks away because almost everything here is within walking distance.

"I should go, I can hear Emma calling me from her kitchen window," Di says. "I'll call again real soon." She hums into the phone. "Actually, not real soon. My Summer Dance Intensive is next week. I'll definitely call when I can, okay?"

When I hang up, I almost start to bawl. Talking to Di only reminded me of how much I miss her. What am I doing so far away from her? Kincardine is great, and I'm having fun here, but it's not home. And I'm not exactly jumping for joy that Di's making all kinds of new friends to take my place while I'm gone. I haven't met anybody here yet. Sure, I see tons of people my age at the beach every day, but I don't know any of them. This isn't like kindergarten, where you can walk up to a group of strange kids and say, "Hi, I'm Penny. Wanna play?" *Boom,* instant friends.

Kalli thumps into the kitchen, dressed only in a bathing suit. She grabs her towel from the coat hook near the sliding door, slips her feet into her sandals, and continues to ignore me as she heads outside.

"Going swimming?"

"Uh huh," she says, sliding the screen closed.

"Can I come?"

She slings the towel over her shoulder. "Not right now. Megan and I are meeting her friend at the picnic shelters. I'll go swimming with you after supper." The sound of her sandals flip-flopping across the deck fades away.

Sandy pads into the kitchen, giving me a soulful look with those huge brown eyes.

"I have to take a number to hang out with my sister," I tell her. "And who's Megan?"

Cocking her head, she looks at me like, "Beats me."

"Want to go for a walk downtown?" I ask.

She runs to the back door, nails clicking noisily, to retrieve her leash from its place in Dad's odds-and-ends basket on the floor. That's another trick I taught her, and in only two days. Sandy races back with the leash in her mouth. I give her the drop command and the leash clatters to the floor at my feet.

"You're such a good puppy," I say, squatting down to give her an affectionate hug and a scratch behind the ears. See, I'm not a loser. I've got a new friend. So what if she has four legs and a tail. Sandy pants happily in my face. Okay, add stinky breath to the list.

Dear Dream Journal,
  Sandy and I have been walking on the beach every morning for a week. I don't know what's going on with me (too much fresh air?), but I've also been jogging

through the cottage lanes at night! I found a dog obedience manual in one of the kitchen drawers, and I study it while at the beach. I'm proud of how well I'm training Sandy to heel beside me as we jog and to ignore distractions, like other dogs, squirrels, kids on bikes, etc. Sometimes when she's trotting along beside me, she'll look up and give me her doggie smile.. That's the coolest.

I don't tell Mom this when I talk to her on the phone, but I'm really happy here.

The headphones to my portable CD player are tangled up in my hair. Guess I fell asleep while listening to Ryan's CD again last night. I tug the headphones free and set them on my dream journal and plastic pencil case. I've got my own small office on the top bunk. Yawning loudly, I stretch out along the wall, my bones popping and cracking like I aged thirty years overnight. I flop over on my other side and come face-to-face with Kalli, who's standing on the bunk bed ladder, gawking at me with eyes so wide her eyebrows have disappeared behind her bangs. But there's a sliver of a smile on her lips.

"What are you doing, you weirdo?" I cry. How often does my whacked-out sister study me while I sleep? Geez!

"I heard you. I heard you talking in another language while you were sleeping. I've been here listening for, like, five minutes. It sounded like Italian or something, and I know you can't speak Italian. You can barely speak English."

"Yeah, right," I say, scuttling down to the end of the bed. I throw my legs over the side and drop to the floor. "If I was talking in my sleep, it was probably gibberish that you thought was a real language. And don't ever watch me again while I sleep, you're creeping me out."

Kalli squawks. "Fine, don't believe me then."

I hate that I have to tilt my head back to look at Kalli. I'm the big sister, damn it.

"I don't believe you. Now let's take Sandy for a walk and get some donuts for breakfast. You in?"

Kalli's tanned arms fold across what little chest she has. "I guess," she concedes.

"Good. Let's get this carb binge going."

As I'm jogging from the room, Kalli mutters, "I know what I heard."

Sandy and I have been jogging for two weeks. I know I'm improving because I don't want to collapse on the sidewalk and die halfway through our route anymore. That's called hitting the wall, Dad told me. Hitting a wall and then getting flattened by an eighteen-wheeler is more like it. Now I know to run right through the wall. There's a secret burst of energy on the other side that keeps me going until we get home.

Our nighttime jog usually starts at eight. I want a lowered chance of people being outside to catch a glimpse of me flailing down the streets like a three-legged cow. I want low lighting for the same reason. But for safety reasons, I want some remaining daylight. Not that anything bad would actually happen to me here, where they have one murder every ten years or so.

Almost every night, as we're nearing the beach playground, we cross paths with another runner. She's got great form, which means she's in way better shape than me, but other than features I can see from a distance, I don't really know what she looks like. I'm new to jogging. Do joggers have a secret camaraderie that involves a passing nod or a wave or a smile or a wink? How should I know? So I basically ignore her, which gets more awkward with each passing night.

Seeing her at the same time and place is fun in a way, like a game between us, but I mostly dread it. My anxiety builds as I near the playground while my brain shouts, *Say hi to her this time, don't say hi, give her a smile at least, just ignore her.* The girl comes bouncing down the street, ponytail bobbing behind her. When she gets close, I veer off to the grass to give her the sidewalk and tell Sandy to *heel* or *ignore*, as if the poor dog is capable of going ballistic and ripping Jogging Girl's legs off. The girl trots past and that's it. My anxiety steamrolls back down to zero.

Tonight, because Kalli and I are going to see a movie, my jog will have to begin at seven. If Jogging Girl and I meet up tonight, that'll mean something fishy is going on, like she's got spies watching me every evening to alert her at the precise moment I lace up my running shoes.

I roll over onto my stomach in my office and grab my dream journal. I scribble: No bad dreams lately. Really tired from jogging. Getting mild shin splints. Must learn to jog properly. Talked to Ryan today. He misses me. I'm dying to go home to see him, but don't want to leave Dad's. Wish I could take Sandy with me. I love her. Think I'll cry when I have to leave. Going for a jog right now.

A low "aroooo-owwrrrr" from Sandy startles me. I peek over the top of my ladder. She's standing in the doorway staring up at me. It cracks me up when she talks. Dad said she didn't do it until I came. She'll walk right up to me and say, "Aroorooo. Urrrrr-rooorrrrrr," like she's making words she thinks I can understand.

"Sandy, there's no way you could know I'm going out tonight and the jog has been moved to seven. Go get your leash," I say, and she skitters away from my bedroom door like a cartoon dog whose speedy legs don't move in sync with its body.

When I'm ready to go, I do a few stretches on the lawn. I always start out slowly to warm up. It's strange to be doing this early, with people around. I feel like I'm running down the street naked and everybody is watching, and booing, and laughing at my wiggling butt. I focus on a point in the distance, a house down the street, and try to forget about possible booers and laughers. I can do this. Breathe in through the nose; breathe out through the mouth. Keep my feet moving. I count my steps to the corner to see if it matches my guess of two hundred steps. It's a hundred and ninety-three.

I'm nearing the playground area. There's no way Jogging Girl will be there at this time, but I'm tensing up anyway. I keep my breathing steady and motor on. The entrance to the playground is about a hundred and twenty steps away. I count inside my head. My anxiety rises. At a hundred and twenty, I pass the playground and exhale deeply in relief. No sign of Jogging Girl. Phew.

"C'mon, Sandy," I say, speeding up. "Let's kick it up a little."

And then I see her, jogging around the next corner, about a

hundred steps away. She's coming, ponytail cheerily bobbing to and fro behind her. My gait falters and I stumble a little, like I've forgotten how to jog even half-assed. When I reach the count of eighty, I hear Jogging Girl speak, hardly out of breath. She says, "You're early tonight."

I glance at her face, for the first time, and give her a quick smile. "You, too."

Over her shoulder, she chuckles and says, "Too weird, huh?"

I look at her again. I get a good hard look. And it spooks the hell out of me.

Jogging Girl is long gone down the street now. And I'm still moving in the opposite direction, slowly. I wind down to a stop, and squat, pretending to tie my shoelaces when really I think I'm going to puke and my legs won't hold me up. I know Jogging Girl's face. I've seen it before. She's Raven, my friend from my dreams.

That's it. I'm absolutely, two hundred percent fed up with all the craziness that's been happening to me since Margie's psychic reading. All the psycho dreams, all the images in my head. I've had it.

I sprint the rest of my jogging route at top speed, my arms pumping hard enough to nearly reach my chin, with Sandy speeding along beside me. She glances up a couple of times to smile at me, as if this is the greatest thing since canned dog food. At the edge of Dad's lawn, my stomach muscles spasm and pain sears through my lungs. I let Sandy off her leash, and she races to her outdoor water bowl while I keel over on the grass. My heart hasn't seen that much action in years. Maybe if I drag myself over to the deck, Sandy will share her water with me before my broiling-hot body spontaneously combusts.

I jog down to the beach on stiffening legs. The lake isn't warm by my impossibly high standards, but I run straight in and plunge into a wave, something I've never done in my life. I sadly drift across the surface on my back and stare at the pink-and-orange sky.

"Let's go. The movie starts in twenty minutes," Kalli says from our bedroom door.

"I'm not going."

"What!" she shrieks.

It takes all my energy to lift my head from my damp pillow. "I'm not going."

"Why? Are you sick?"

"Sort of."

Big sigh. "Fine. I'll go see if Megan can go with me." She thumps away.

I think I'll lie here on the top bunk and stare at the ceiling for the rest of my life. I'm sure Dad won't mind. The hygiene level up here might get a little grotesque after a year or two, but who cares. I'm here for the long haul.

"Rooooooooo."

"I'm not coming down, Sandy."

"Aroooooo-rooo-roo," she says from the doorway.

"No. Now go lie down."

Sandy whines and pads away from the room. I wonder if she wants to hop on the bed with me but can't because I'm too high up. I've heard that pets can sense your moods. Can she tell I've crumbled down to a fine layer of dust inside?

Dad is walking toward my room now. His footsteps sound different from Kalli's.

"Kalli says you're not going to the movie."

"That's right."

He doesn't say anything. I silently count to ten, hoping he'll go away so I can go back to wallowing in my craziness in peace.

"Penny, I know it's kind of boring here," Dad says quietly. "If you miss your mom and your friends, and want to go home early, that's okay. Just let me know."

I stare at the ceiling, counting and ignoring . . . sixty-one, sixty-two, sixty-three. I continue to count until I hear Dad and Kalli talking in the kitchen.

Over and over in my head, I ask myself, *do I want to go home?* And the more I say it, the closer my answer moves to yes.

It's eleven-thirty in the morning. I still haven't left my perch on the top bunk. That makes fifteen hours straight, and if I don't figure out a way to rig up a waste management system in the next ten minutes, I'll be scraping pieces of my bladder off the walls.

"Kalli!" I holler.

"What?" she yells back from the living room.

"Get me a bucket, a funnel, and seven feet of rubber hose!"

"Yeah, right. Get off your fat butt and get your own bucket and hose."

Damn. I can't believe I might have to end my reign as Bunk-Bed Queen after only fifteen hours. Fifteen hours isn't even close to forever. I hustle down the ladder and race to the bathroom. When I finally emerge, feeling about ten pounds lighter, Kalli is leaning against the wall in the hallway.

"Dad thinks you don't like it here," she says, scowling. "I knew you'd screw this up."

"I'm not screwing anything up." I walk into our room, hoping she'll leave, but knowing she'll follow me like a tall, boob-less shadow.

As I'm climbing the bunk-bed ladder, Kalli says, "Don't you dare make us leave early, Penny. All the kids here like me. I'm cool, not like at home, where all the idiot guys call me Stork. If you make us leave early, I'll never forgive you. Ever."

At the top rung, I stop climbing and turn around. Kalli's cheeks go bright pink. She stares at her bare feet.

I take a deep breath and exhale slowly. "We're not leaving early. I'm just thinking about some stuff, that's all."

Kalli hesitates. "Okay. It's supposed to thunderstorm today. Wanna rent a movie?"

Rent a movie or rot in bed? Tough choice. "Ask me again later."

ZZZ

Dear Dream Journal:

Last night I dreamed that Ryan and I were at a toga party. Finally, a fun dream! We were both completely hammered because there was this fountain in the middle of the party that spewed out wine. Who could resist that? When I woke up, I missed him really bad. I had to climb down from bed to call him. Should have checked out the time first, though. His mom didn't exactly appreciate my six-thirty wake-up call. Whoops.

I'm lying in the top bunk. No surprise there. I've spent roughly sixty percent of my time here in the last five days. There's not much to do up here, other than write in my dream journal and listen to Ryan's CD over and over. I've got every song memorized.

I've also been thinking way more than usual, and I can't figure out why Dad decided to become the husband Mom needs but can no longer have. I love the caring, sensitive person he is now. We came this close to being the perfect family, but Dad screwed it all up by deciding to change his ways a few years too late.

If my parents had stayed together, would I be a different person now? Would I like myself more or less? If Mom had met the man of her dreams, I wouldn't exist. Di would have a different best friend and Ryan would have a different girlfriend.

It's scary to realize that I influence the lives of other people, even people I don't know. Say my shoe comes untied while I'm jogging. Scenario One: I stop to tie it. A cyclist cruises around the corner, swerves to avoid a collision with me, and is killed by a car. In two seconds, I've changed the course of my life and the lives of every person the cyclist knew. Scenario Two: I jog out of the way to tie my shoe, the cyclist lives and later gives birth to a future Nobel Prize-winning physicist. Or a serial killer.

If destiny is real, and life is like a script to follow, what happens if I'm meant to tie my shoe, but I decide against it? The whole movie would have to be rewritten from that point on. Everything would change.

The more I think about it, the less I want to leave the top bunk.

I dig a trench into the cool sand with the heel of my foot, listening to waves crash onto the shore. I feel like I need toothpicks to prop my heavy eyelids open, that's how tired I am. I spend a lot of time in bed, but I'm sure not getting much sleep while I'm there.

"Penny, you've never been to the sea!" Kalli says, in the exasperated voice she talks to me with when Megan's around.

My stinging heel takes a break. "I never said I have. What are you talking about?"

Kalli and Megan look at each other, conversing with their eyes. Then they turn their eyes to me, to let me know they've silently reached their verdict. I'm nuts.

"Didn't you hear yourself talking?" Kalli says. "You said,

'The waves remind me of the sea.' That's what you said, totally, word for word. Right, Megan?"

Megan nods. "That's what you said, Penelope. I've been to the sea and the waves don't sound like this."

I wish the pipsqueak wouldn't call me by my full name. And I'm not in the mood for this lame prank they're pulling.

"You got me," I say, playing along to shut them up. "I've never been to the sea."

"Hey, Kalli, let's sit in the water and let the waves smash into us!" Megan shouts, the best idea she's had all day.

They scramble up and brush off. The wind carries the sand directly to my mouth.

"No swimming. It's a yellow-flag day," I say, and sand grits between my teeth. Thunder rumbles in the distance. I gauge the swollen clouds that now hide the sun. "Fifteen more minutes and then we'll have to go home."

"I know, I know."

Kalli and Megan bop down to the shore. Even with her puffy curls, Megan is head and shoulders shorter than my sister. Pointing out the approaching big waves, they sit at the water's edge. Right away, a swell of whitecapped water whacks into them. Megan gets the brunt of it in the face, and they both fall over backwards. They struggle to sitting and prepare for the next onslaught, shrieking like they're on an amusement park ride.

My wobbling head settles back on my shoulder blades. It's not the most comfortable position, but I don't want to move. I close my eyes and breathe slowly. Quiet thunder rolls across the sky, far off, like a giant is shaking and rippling a blanket of air. Waves build and crash.

The waves remind me of the sea.

I relax into the rising and falling sounds, comforted.

The sea is strong, Astrid. Help me.

"Penelope!"

I shake awake. For a split second, I don't know where I am. The sky over the horizon has darkened to a scary green-gray. The cool breeze has picked up to a gust. It whips tiny bullets of sand at my bare skin. Lightning ignites a monstrous cloud over the far side of the lake.

Megan runs over, soaking wet. "Kalli needs you!"

"Where is she?" I say, at the same time the thunder reaches us.

"Over there. She can't get out!"

I leap to my feet and run, searching the waves. In the waist-deep water between the shore and the sandbar, Kalli fights to get back to the beach, not making any progress.

"Kalli, relax! You're panicking!" I call out. "Don't try to walk straight in."

Her arms flail and she slips under the water. I want to run in and pull her out. My instincts are keeping me from doing that. She bounces back up and regains her footing, still waist-deep, but farther away than I was expecting.

"Penny, what do I do? It's sucking on me!"

I run down the beach until I'm in line with her, and point

toward the cottage. "Swim that way, to the side! Then swim diagonally, not straight in!"

For the first time ever, Kalli listens to me. Her body crests a wave like a surfboard. She paddles hard, even though she must be tired. I keep pace with her on land, until I reach Megan, who shivers next to me, cocooned inside her beach towel.

Kalli's doing exactly as I told her; swimming crossways. I run into the lake and hold out my hand, anxious to catch her. Below the surface, the current grips my legs. I loosen the sand with my feet and anchor myself into the muck. A cresting wave carries Kalli to me, and I grab a handful of her bathing suit. We drag each other onto the beach.

"Are you okay?" I say, relieved but wanting to clobber her for scaring me like that.

Her lower lip shakes. I never noticed how much she still looks like a kid.

"That was the scariest thing ever. Worse than ripping my pants at Sam Pratt's party."

I pick up her towel and hand it to her. "C'mon. Unless we want to get fried by lightning, we need to go inside."

She and Megan trail along behind me, chattering.

Under the cover of the tree-lined path, my anger hits its boiling point. "You know, I can't believe you were dumb enough to do that," I say, spinning around to face them. "I specifically told you not to go swimming."

"A wave sucked me out when I was sitting down," she says, crying. "I called to you, lots of times, but you ignored me."

I wince. "Oh man, Kalli, I'm sorry. I must have fallen asleep."

"It's okay." She snorts back a sniffle and wipes her eyes with her towel. "You knew exactly what to do to save me."

A clap of thunder booms overhead. It seems to split the swollen clouds open at the seams, and we race to the cottage to take cover. We soak the kitchen floor and joke about what happened. We all got out of it safe and sound.

If only I could stop thinking about what Kalli said. How did I know what to do to help her, anyway? I have absolutely no idea.

10

I'm back to normal, as normal as I can get anyway, which means I use the top bunk when it's dark outside, not round the clock. But I can't get back into jogging. I don't want to run into Jogging Girl again. I don't understand all the weird things that keep happening to me, and if I stay away from Jogging Girl, I can pretend the dreams and my real life don't coincide. It's all too bizarre.

Right now Kalli and I are watching TV. Dad is in the kitchen. I can hear him banging pots around, cleaning up the supper dishes.

"Kalli, you should help Dad clean up." I sigh, stretching out to hog the whole couch.

Without glancing away from the TV, she says, "F-you."

A commercial I hate comes on. I lug myself up from the couch.

Dad stops drying a glass to give me a smile. "Taking Sandy for a run?"

Sandy, splayed out on the kitchen floor, glances up at me, moving only her eyeballs.

"Yeah, I guess I will," I say, surprising myself. "I'll help you clean up first."

"Oh, no, you don't. Get out there and go for a run." He swishes the dishtowel at me.

All of a sudden, I'm pumped about going for a jog. But I'm still nervous about seeing Jogging Girl. I don't want to think about how Dad came to live in the same town as somebody I've dreamed about. That's one more coincidence I don't want to deal with.

"Dad, why did you move here?" *Hey, you don't want to think about that, remember?*

"Because I was offered a job here."

"Yeah, I know. I guess what I'm saying is, how did the job offer come about?"

Dad puts the clean glass away and shuts the cupboard door. "It was good luck, that's what it was. A friend of mine, Mark Talford, who I hadn't seen since I was still with Mom, called me up out of the blue last year. He's a supervisor at the plant here."

"He got you the job?"

"Yeah." Leaning against the counter, Dad says, "Everything came together at the right time." He shrugs and goes back to washing dishes. "Getting the job and the chance to move here were the best things that could have happened to me. It was meant to be."

It was meant to be.

Silverware slips from Dad's soapy hands and clatters into the sink, splashing bubbles all over the counter. I grab a dry dishtowel from the oven door handle and throw it to him. When he turns to catch it, his face is red and he won't meet my gaze.

Talking about this is upsetting Dad for some reason. I stare at the floor, counting the tile squares. Is it because he had to leave us to be happy in life?

"Well," Dad exclaims, startling me. "I think there's a doggie here who's waiting very patiently for a certain homebody to take her jogging."

What doesn't kill you makes you stronger, but when things got tough, I went and hid out on the top bunk. I can't stop living my life just in case something strange happens to me.

"Sandy, get your leash," I say, and she excitedly hurries to standing, her pink tongue lolling out through a big dog smile.

I can do this.

As I'm approaching the entrance to the beach playground, I nearly burst out laughing. All I had to do to avoid running into Jogging Girl was jog to somewhere else. Okay, I never claimed to be a genius. And, with my luck, she would have changed her route to match mine and we'd pass each other anyway.

I check my watch. It's a little after eight. When I glance up, I fully expect to see Jogging Girl come bouncing around the corner at the end of the street. But she doesn't materialize. Sandy and I trot to the corner. Still no girl. We've never made it this far without meeting her. As a test of the Emergency Telepathy Broadcast System, I yell inside my head, *Hey, Jogging Girl. I'm out for a jog. Bring it on.*

I count my footfalls. At two hundred, I start to get tense. Where is she? Is she sick? Didn't she receive my telepathic message? Does she actually have a life, unlike me?

There's a gradual downhill slope at the end of this street, which gives me a chance to catch my breath. It's only about a hundred steps away. Thinking about the hill is the one thing that keeps me going up to this point in the jog. My leg muscles relax to take me down the hill nice and easy. Taking advantage of the sudden ease of running, I inhale a few deep breaths to refill my oxygen stores for a while.

Halfway down the hill, I hear a girl call out, "Hey, you're back."

The voice came from the other side of the street, and it can only be one person. I jog a few more steps, wondering what I should do.

Sandy, unfortunately, decides for me. In an uncharacteristic display of bad behavior, she darts behind me, practically wrenching my arm out of its socket. Legs kicking out, I struggle to hold Sandy back as she drags me into the path of an oncoming car. Lucky for me, the car is now driving well below the town's Old Lady speed limit, so the driver can better observe my amusing display of dorkiness. Jogging Girl's still there, staring at me with wide eyes. Her mouth does this hilarious grimace to the side.

"Sandy, no!" I holler, but I'm fighting to contain a fit of hysterical giggling. There's no way the dumb dog will take me seriously. I yank hard on her leash and wrestle her back to the sidewalk, yelling, "Sandy, *sit*! Sit! I said *sit*! Sit *down*!"

Sandy's tongue flops out through her open, grinning mouth and she plants her butt on the sidewalk. I am never, ever, ever having kids.

Jogging Girl glances right and left to check for cars and

then does this super-athletic walk to cross the street. A super-athletic walk that's leading her straight to me. I quickly check out the street she came from, a tree-lined side street that disappears into what I call a Minivan Neighborhood. Everybody drives a minivan, the kids have stay-at-home moms, the lawns are mowed regularly by cute dads who wear suits during the week and baseball caps, jeans, and T-shirts on the weekends.

"Sorry," Jogging Girl says, stepping up to the curb. She holds her hand out for Sandy to sniff. "I didn't know your dog would do that."

"Neither did I." I smile. Breathe, breathe, breathe. Keep the manic giggles safely locked away.

It's even harder to act normal when I look into Jogging Girl's huge almond-shaped eyes, so brown they remind me of chocolate. Her face and lips are fuller than Raven's, but her eyes are identical. My mental image of her isn't coming from a dream memory this time. I feel like I've spent years staring into Jogging Girl's face.

"I'm Katherine," she says. "Actually, I'm only Katherine to my mom. Everybody else calls me Kate."

"I'm Penelope. To my mom, when she's angry. Everybody else calls me Penny."

Kate pulls her ponytail tight. "I'm going for a run. Is it okay if I join you, Penny?"

Oh, great. It was easy to pretend to be a good runner around Jogging Girl before. I only had to put on my act for the one minute we were in each other's sight. I don't like the idea of running with accompaniment, and it seems a little strange to me that Kate wants to jog with me in the first place. She doesn't even know me.

"Sure, you can come. But I'm not sure if I'll be able to keep up with you."

"Of course you will," she says, with an exaggerated swish of her hand. "You're already warmed up, which means you're probably running about eight miles an hour, whereas I'm just starting out, which means I'll be running at about six miles an hour. If anything, I'll have trouble keeping up with you."

Okaaaaay. Jogging Girl is quite possibly the oddest person I've ever met. Cool.

In sync, we jog and talk for about twenty minutes. Actually, I don't do much talking; I'm too busy trying to breathe. Kate takes care of most of the conversation, and she has interesting things to say. When we near Dad's street, I contemplate running past it, not wanting to go home yet. But Sandy knows our route and she turns the corner, dragging me onto our street.

"This is where I live," I say, and we jog to a stop in front of Dad's place.

"Feel like coming over to my place to hang for a while?" Kate asks. She shrugs, like it's no big deal if I say no, but I can see in her face that she'd like me to come over.

"Sure, I'll come over. Just let me take Sandy into the house and tell my dad."

Kate waits for me at the edge of the yard. I race toward the cottage, beaming like crazy. Boom. Instant friends.

How was I supposed to know Jogging Girl's post-jogging routine occasionally involves getting drunk? When we got up to her bedroom and Kate asked me if I wanted a drink, I said sure, thinking she'd return with juice or water or milk. Instead, she came back with soda of the hazardous-waste variety.

"Your room's really nice, Kate."

"Puleeeeze," she says, rolling her eyes. She chugs her drink and drags a hand across her full lips. One thing I like about Kate is that every move she makes is exaggerated. She's like a stage actress. "My mother had professional painters come in to do my room. This is my mom's I-wish-I-were-a-teenager-again room. If I had my way, the whole room would be lime green with mathematical equations hand-scrawled across the walls. And I'd load every wall with Pre-Raphaelite paintings."

Taking a chance on embarrassing myself, I ask, "What's a Pre-Raphaelite painting?"

"Pre-Raphaelite means before Raphael. The Pre-Raphaelites used a lot of nature in their paintings. They wanted to create art the way it was before Raphael."

Wow, Kate's smart. Art-smart like Diana.

"I have a journal with a Dali painting on it," I say.

"Dali's cool. Totally whacked, but cool. What's your favorite Dali painting?"

Uh oh. "*Persistence of Memory,*" I say nonchalantly, like I know a whole bunch of Dali paintings and chose that particular one after great deliberation.

"His trompe l'oeil paintings are my favorites."

We've entered into foreign language territory. I think I'll let this conversation die.

"How old are you?" I ask, studying Kate's face.

"I'm two hundred months old."

Is that math right? Beats the hell outta me. I just nod and sip my drink.

"I'll be seventeen on Halloween," she says, laughing at me. "An old wives' tale says that people born on Halloween are able to see and talk to spirits. If I wasn't afraid of ghosts, I'd give that a try."

"Not me. I've seen enough movies to know I don't want to see a ghost."

"You like horror movies?"

"I do. But they scare me."

In the middle of taking a sip, Kate sputters and coughs. "That's the point." She wipes her chin with the corner of her floral comforter. "Do you like photography?"

Do I like photography? What kind of question is that? If she means do I enjoy getting my picture taken, the answer is an emphatic no.

"We have a darkroom downstairs," she says. "I'm obsessed with taking pictures."

My brain on vodka immediately associates sex with

whatever it is Kate just said. Something about taking pictures, do I like photography, I have a darkroom.

"You have a darkroom? In your house?"

"Doesn't everyone?" Kate smirks and takes a drink. "Photography is my dad's life, when he's at work and when he's not. You saw the framed photos on the way upstairs?"

I couldn't have missed them. They took up most of the wall. "Your dad took them?"

"We both did," she says. "I've always wanted to be just like my dad. But my mom thinks a bright girl like me should be a lawyer or a surgeon. Or a Director of Nursing, like her. Those are important jobs. By important, she means they pay more money than the 'artsy-fartsy job' I'll really end up doing. I could have gotten out of this town a year ago, if my parents had let me skip second grade."

"You were supposed to skip a grade? Are you really smart?"

"That's what my mom likes to think. I think that I was an annoying little smart-ass, and my teacher just wanted to get me the hell out of her class."

"I see," I say, playing along. "Your high school grades must suck, right, since you're not smart and all."

"They're okay. Mid-nineties."

I spit a mouthful of vodka-and-soda back into my glass. "I didn't know there were grades that high," I say, but inside I'm thinking, *I thought only brown-nosed geeks got grades that high.* "Do you study a lot?"

"Hell, no." Kate slurps back a big gulp, crunches an ice cube between her teeth. "I hate studying. It's boring. When I take a test, I can see my notes in my mind. If I couldn't do that, my grades would be shit."

Wish I was born with superhuman abilities like that, I think, taking another drink. The muscles in my shoulders prickle. I rub my temple, feeling lightheaded and giddy already.

"Do you have a boyfriend?" I ask. I glance around her professionally decorated room, wondering where the bathroom is.

"No," she says. "I'd rather have a pet leech."

We stare into each other's eyes and burst out laughing at the same time.

"The kids here in Kincardine," Kate says in a mature voice, "all they want to do is party. That's all they think there is to do in this boring town, screw their boyfriends and get drunk." She shakes her head. "I'm above all that."

We both glance at our nearly empty mugs and start laughing again.

Soda bubbles tickle my tongue. Vodka burns my throat, and I swallow quickly. "You know that Raphael guy?" I tentatively ask.

"Not personally."

"Did he die young?" I feel silly right away for asking, but I have to know.

"A morbid question. I love it," Kate says, setting her glass on the floor. She jumps up and grabs a massive book from the bookcase beside her bed. "He did die young. All the books mention that, how short his life was. He was one of the Master painters of the High Renaissance, you know, taught by Michelangelo and Leonardo."

Kate lays the book out and flips crazily through the pages. "Here he is," she says, sliding the book across the floor so I can see it. "See this painting? It's called the *Madonna Sixtina*, or *Sistine Madonna*. It's one of his most famous ones." She points to two boy angels resting their chins on their arms at the bottom of the painting. "You've probably only seen that part of the painting before, right?"

"I've seen them on lots of stuff. I didn't know they were part of a famous painting, though." I study the Madonna. She's standing on a layer of clouds above the angels. "She's pretty."

Kate puts her face close to the book. She looks at me. Her face zooms back to the book. "Well, it's no wonder you think she's pretty. You look just like her."

"I do not," I say, making a dorky face.

"You do, too." Kate jumps up again and strides over to her desk. Art supplies clatter across the desktop, pencils fly. She races back with a rosy red pencil. "Raphael made his women's mouths too small," she says, rolling her eyes. Evidently she has a problem with the Master. "I'll shade the mouth out a little. And keep in mind that a portrait isn't really like a photograph. An artist does his own interpretation of a face."

With a few deft touches of the pencil, Kate fills out the Madonna's mouth. I may not have seen a resemblance between the woman in the painting and myself before, but I can't deny it now. I'm staring up at myself from the book, from a painting—I check the dates beside Raphael's picture—that's almost five hundred years old.

I look up, and Kate is staring quizzically at my face. "Wow, that's eerie," she says.

"You know what's really eerie?"

"What?" Kate says, breathless.

I point to the blond-haired woman kneeling beside the Madonna. "She looks like my best friend, Diana."

 It's school picture day.
The line moves through the gym, one person at a time. Finally it's my turn. I take a seat and nervously clasp my hands on my lap.

"You are perfection!" the photographer shouts, and I nearly teeter off the stool. His brown hair is held back in a ponytail and he's wearing a tweed jacket and jeans. He tilts his head this way and that to scrutinize my face. "I want you."

At the end of the line, Di steps out into view, her mouth set in a hard grimace. She looks ticked off about something, that's for sure.

The photographer takes my hand. "I must do your portrait. Come with me."

There's no way I want to go anywhere with him. Something about him is making me nervous—an inner fervor that's locked away, waiting to come out. I can see it in his eyes.

I shake my head. "I think I'll stay here."

"No, no, no," he says, tugging me up from the stool. "You are the one I want."

Unable to stop myself, I follow him. I glance toward the end of the line, hoping Diana can help me.

She glowers at me, whirls around, and strides to the door. It flies open and crashes into the wall. I watch, unable to call out, as Di races away down the hall.

When I turn to do something about the weird photographer, I discover I'm no longer in the gym. I'm being led down a narrow cobblestone street at dusk. I nearly trip on the uneven stones beneath my feet.

I feel an overwhelming sense of being home. We're in Travestere. My father owns a bakery down the street, in the square. The river, the Tiber, I can hear it. Fig trees stretch their gnarled branches over the stone garden wall beside me. I smell Father's bread baking. And there's the Santa Maria church.

The photographer stops walking. He glides his hands up my arms. "I cannot take another step without making love to you, Margherita."

Kissing my neck, he backs me down the street and into a dark alley. I turn to soft clay in his skilled hands.

Bang!

I startle awake, almost bouncing off the bed. "What was that?"

"Sorry. Kicked bunk-bed ladder," Kalli mumbles sleepily.

Nice timing. That photographer guy sure knew what he was doing.

Dear Dream Journal:
Last night I had a dream about a crazy photographer, and I realized he looked like Raphael from Kate's art

book. I'm not sure if he's the Raphael I've already dreamed about or if I put him in a dream because I saw him in the book. At the end of the dream, it felt like I stopped being me and became the woman in the dream. I knew what she was thinking and seeing.

I spend my days being me, but I spend my nights being someone else. And the scary thing is, the dream part seems almost as real to me as life does when I'm awake. It's like I'm living a double life.

Kate shows up unannounced outside Dad's patio door while I'm slumped over the table, shoveling cereal into my mouth. My hair is sticking out like I spent the night in a tornado and my pajamas consist of a stretched-out Pink Floyd shirt I stole from Ryan and a pair of ratty boxer shorts. Maybe I should have given Kate my phone number. I'm not real big on surprises.

With my spoon dangling from my mouth, I wave her inside with one hand and straighten out my hair with the other. When the door slides open, Sandy barrels into the kitchen from the living room, nearly colliding with Kate and the dishwasher.

"Hi, it's hot as hell out there. Let's go. The beach is calling our names."

I stick my spoon back in the bowl. "Okay, give me a couple minutes." My cereal's too mushy. I set the bowl on the floor for Sandy. "Want something to eat?"

"No, thanks, I already had a bowl of soggy cereal and dog drool."

"I mean toast or waffles or something," I say, laughing.

"No, I'm okay. My mom made me some chocolate chip pancakes."

Saliva washes into my mouth like the tide coming in. Chocolate chip pancakes. Now that's the kind of breakfast I could go for. Where can I get a mom like Kate's?

"You can watch TV, nobody's here but me," I say, gesturing toward the living room. "I'll get ready real quick."

"No hurry," Kate says, collapsing onto the sofa.

I yank on my bathing suit, do as much as I can to become presentable without having a shower, and grab my bag of beach gear.

At the beach, we lay my blanket out on the hot sand.

For some reason, I figured Kate to be a one-piece, cover-as-much-skin-as-possible bathing suit gal like myself. But, nope, she wiggles out of her shorts and whips off her tank top to expose a whole lot of epidermis. I don't think the teeny cotton triangles would even classify as a bathing suit. More like a *bath su*. And she must lift weights, in addition to running. Her abs and biceps are totally cut and she looks strong enough to pick my dad up and whirl him around over her head, Pippi Longstocking–style.

I take off my shorts, leave my T-shirt on, and stretch out on my back. Kate pulls a tattered book from her bag and takes a seat beside me. Instead of reading, though, she fires off a ton of questions about my friends, my school, my town, my family, my boyfriend, and my hobbies. She pretty much asks me everything but my bra size, which she has probably already deduced by looking at me. If it were anybody else heaping personal questions on me, I'd definitely get creeped out. But I don't mind giving the answers to Kate. It's even a little fun.

"Okay, you passed the test. I deem you worthy," she says, fanning herself with her book, a copy of *Animal Farm*, I notice. "Any questions you want to ask me?"

I turn on my side and give her a one-shoulder shrug. "You like Pink Floyd?"

"Of course."

"Okay, you passed the test. I deem you worthy."

"I noticed your T-shirt this morning," Kate says. "You like Pink Floyd? For real?"

"I'm a Pink Floyd addict."

"Next time you're in my room, I'll show you something," she says with a chuckle.

I suddenly get wistful for Ryan, like some sappy girl in a melodramatic romance novel. I roll onto my stomach and rest my chin on my arms, wishing I could talk to him more often.

"I went through my art books," Kate says. "You're in a bunch of other paintings."

"I'm telling you, that girl doesn't look like me," I say. "Want to go for swim?"

"She does too. Well, you with a bit of a thyroid problem. But otherwise, she looks like she could be your great-great-great—okay, a lot of greats, grandmother."

I open my mouth to change the subject.

"The thing is," Kate says, "up until Raphael moved to Rome, the girls in his paintings were these scrawny blond chicks, because that was the type of girl everybody loved, how truly pathetic that nothing has changed in five hundred years, and women used to, even back then, dye their hair blond or wear blond wigs, and—"

"What happened after he moved to Rome?" I blurt at the first opening I get.

"After that, the women in his paintings became chubbier, olive-skinned girls with dark hair and dark eyes. It's like he was using the same model over and over."

"Oh." I turn my head and watch two little girls build a sand castle at the water's edge.

Kate lies on her back and cracks open the book, holding it high to shield her face from the sun. "Do you want to come over to my place this afternoon?" she asks, after reading through a few pages.

The prospect of checking out Kate's art books doesn't sound very appealing. I give a noncommittal groan. The warm sunshine zaps my energy, and my eyes slip closed.

◆◆
◆ I'm nude. Not completely naked, but the gauzy veil draped across my middle isn't covering a portion of my body that it definitely should be covering.

Raphael steps out from behind his easel, and I yank the veil higher. Why's he painting me naked! He must be some kind of pervert.

"Keep that smile," he says. "It is perfect."

Smile! That's sheer terror and embarrassment on my face. Just when I'm about to wake myself up, something glitters, catching my attention. I stretch my hand out. It's a ring. And not just any ring either, it's a monster, the most gigantic ruby I've ever seen. It dwarfs my ring finger.

From behind the canvas, Raphael says, "Penny, you should wake up now. You're getting sunburned."

"What?"

"Wake up, girl," he calls out. "Your face is frying."

I open my eyes.

"Flip over, Penny," Kate says. "You're well done on top and rare on the bottom, and nobody likes a half-cooked burger."

Still half-asleep, I flop over onto my stomach.

"Let's go get some ice cream. I'm buying." Kate sits up, folds the corner of the page in her book, and sticks it back in her bag. "Then we'll go to my house."

It's unacceptable to turn down free ice cream. I lumber to standing and pull on my shorts. After I gather up my beach stuff, we walk over to Dad's to deposit it on the deck. Kalli, back from a sleepover, walks out the patio door with Megan in tow. Megan's so dainty and cute. It's a shame she comes with an extraordinarily high annoyance factor.

"Some man just dropped off a box for you," Kalli says. "I put it on the table."

"A box. What's in it?"

Hopping down the deck steps, she says, "Like I know. The box is long and skinny."

Megan leans over, shielding her mouth with her hand and whispers something in Kalli's ear. I overhear the word "vibrator." Oh, she's such a delight, that Megan. She and Kalli run off, their megaphone mouths blaring nonsense and shrill giggles.

Inside the kitchen, I find the box on the table. What a doughhead Kalli is. The name of the florist shop is displayed right on the lid of the box. I open it up.

"Roses. Who are they from?" Kate asks. She whips the mini-envelope out of my hand and holds it to her forehead, squinting hard in concentration. "The answer is: the guy who hasn't been able to get in your pants yet."

Embarrassed, I grab the envelope and pop it open. "Wish You Were Here—Ryan."

"Nice." Kate's elbow jabs my arm. "Any guy who makes references to Pink Floyd albums when he sends flowers is all right by me."

"Nobody's ever given me flowers before," I admit. I have such a great boyfriend, and I can't see him for a month. At this moment, a month might as well be a year.

I put the flowers in the vase they came with and set them on the kitchen table.

"Aren't they beautiful?"

"Sure," Kate says. "If you're into flowers and junk."

I narrow my eyes at her and she laughs.

"You know what else is beautiful?" she asks, leading me to the patio door. "Rocky Road ice cream."

We walk downtown, behaving like an older version of Kalli

and Megan. When we get close to the ice cream parlor, my shoulders tense up.

"Uh, I just remembered I can't get ice cream here unless I order in a Scottish accent."

Kate snorts. Staring me straight in the eye, she says, "What do you want?" She doesn't even ask me to explain the Scottish accent thing. I tell her what kind I want and she strolls away, reaching deep into the pocket of her shorts.

"Hello, there," the woman in the parlor calls. "How's the vacation going?"

My shoulders crank a little tighter. I glance up to see her smiling at me, elbow deep in a bucket of ice cream.

"Super," I say, and it rolls off my tongue like melting Scottish butter.

Kate gives me an amused grin over her shoulder. She's loving this, I can tell. With both cones in her hands, she strides back to me.

"Have a nice afternoon," the ice cream woman says, and this time I just wave.

I take my cone from Kate. My sunburned cheeks glow like neon signs.

"Thanks for the ice cream." I'm back to being non-Scottish.

Kate's tongue whirls around her ice cream and she bites the peak off. "Nuuuuu problem, lassie."

The amount of time it takes to walk from the middle of downtown to Kate's house is exactly how long it takes to eat an ice cream cone from start to finish.

"C'mon upstairs," Kate says, wiping her hands on the back of her shorts. "I'll take out my art books." She winks. "And I'll expose my room's deep, dark secret."

Kate shuts the bedroom door behind us and motions for me to take a seat on her neatly made bed, which I do.

"See this cork bulletin board," she announces, striking a game-show hostess pose to showcase the board's notes and photos and reminders.

She grabs the board down from the wall and turns it around. The back of the board is completely covered in Pink Floyd photos and memorabilia.

"My whole room is reversible. One side of this board goes with the My Mom Reliving Her Teen Years theme. The other side is the real me." At the window, she tugs on the window-blind cord and the slats rotate shut. "These blinds appear to be plain, old, boring white." With a yank to the opposite cord, the blind slats flip over to reveal a colorful and remarkable painted collage. Trees, stars, cats, sections of sheet music, black and white reproductions of photos, and many other images that mean nothing to me, but must have great significance to Kate, fill the window frame.

I shake my head in awe. "That's intense. You painted that?"

"Yeah," she says, smiling. "There's more, though."

Around the room she goes, pointing out all the things that are reversible. Each one takes me by surprise. She turns her back to me, gathering her hair up. The section of hair at the base of her neck, visible only when all her hair is up, has been dyed alternating strips of purple and lime green. I've seen her hair in a ponytail plenty of times, but only from the front as she jogged past.

"That's wicked," I say. "Does your mom know about your secrets and reversibles?"

Kate lets her hair fall back around her shoulders. "Some." She walks over to her bookshelf. "She definitely doesn't know which body parts I've had pierced."

My eyebrows shoot up. Wherever Kate's piercings are, they're not visible to the naked eye.

She pulls out the same big book she showed me the last time I was here, and I cringe as she flips through the pages on her way toward me, her eyebrows furrowed tight with determination. She sets the book on my lap, open to the one painting I don't want to see. I don't want to know that it's real.

"There she is." Her finger stabs the nude woman draped in a veil. "That's the same girl we saw in the other painting. Who is she? That's what I want to know."

I want to look away, but I can't. Something about the painting is off. It's wrong. Then in a flash it comes to me. "Where's her ring?" I cry.

Kate spears me with a look that's filled with curiosity. "Say what?"

Damn. My big mouth strikes again. "Nothing," I say with a nonchalant shrug.

"No way. Tell me what ring you're talking about."

I inhale deeply. "It's nothing. Forget I said that."

"I ain't forgetting nothin'. I'm getting the willies all of a sudden and you're going to tell me what you mean, or I'm"— Kate holds up the book—"I'm going to show this nekked picture of you to every single person I know."

This makes me laugh, despite being angry at my big mouth. "I'll tell, but promise me you won't think I'm weird."

"It's too late, I already think that. Now tell me about the ring, or this picture of your boobs is getting scanned into my computer. You'll be Internet porn within a matter of minutes."

"Okay, fine. It's a huge, square ruby ring. Are you satisfied?"

Kate throws the book over her shoulder and leaps off the bed. At her desk, she whacks the computer mouse and clicks and clacks noisily on the keyboard.

"What are you doing?"

"I'm putting the words *Raphael* and *ruby ring* into a search engine."

I freeze in the middle of getting up from the bed.

Kate leans close to the monitor, intent on reading an article she's brought up on the screen. Slowly, she turns around to look at me. "Did you already read about that painting or see something on the news about it?"

"Why?" I ask, wishing I could zip back in time. I should have said no to the free ice cream and stayed at the beach. I should have kept my big stupid mouth shut.

"Come look at this."

I unwillingly move closer to the computer.

"This article says there is a ruby ring, possibly an engagement ring, on her finger." A flicker of excitement goes through Kate's eyes. "A couple of months ago, they did an X-ray on the painting to restore it, and found the ring, hidden under a layer of paint."

I swallow hard, but my mouth has gone almost dry.

"There was a ring on her finger, just like you said. It was kept secret for almost five hundred years. So how did you know it was there?"

I shrug, not knowing what to say. Lies never spring to my mouth when I need them. My silence drags out for way too long. I could leave without telling Kate about the ring, but I have the feeling she'd tackle me to the ground on my mad dash to the door.

"It's pretty strange," I say.

"Of course it is. That's why I want to know."

I can't spontaneously explain it to Kate, here and now, and expect everything to come out coherently. "Can I tell you later? I need some time to think about what to say."

Kate breathes out through her nose, loudly, like Sandy does when she's bored. Her lips press tight. We stare into each other's eyes.

"I guess," she says. "But don't think I'll forget. I'll pester you constantly. You'll rue the day you asked me to wait. It might take a whole lotta liquor, but I'll get you to talk." She points a finger at me, squinting mischievously. "I know where you live."

The tightness in my chest relaxes. "Yeah, yeah. I get the picture."

◆◆
◆ Diana strolls into the room where I'm modeling for
Raphael. The close fit of her fur-trimmed velvet gown
accentuates her beautiful figure and a jeweled caul holds her
blond hair off her pale face.

My hands clench as she crosses the room.

"Maria, how lovely to see you," Raphael says to her.

"Will you not greet your fiancée with a kiss!" she says, coyly,
and Raphael steps out from behind the canvas to give her a peck
on the cheek. "Please ask Margherita to excuse us."

Holding back my anger, I hurry from the room and close the
door. When I turn to leave, my arm knocks against a wooden
table. I study the objects neatly laid out before me: An open bottle of red wine, a wineglass, a shallow bowl of paint pigment,
and a note.

On the note, written in a spiral pattern around skull and
crossbones, are the words "Orpiment: Do Not Eat, Do Not
Drink, Do Not Touch." I scoop up a pea-sized amount of the
bright yellow pigment. Into the wineglass it goes. I fill the glass
with the blood-red liquid and swirl to mix. Glass in hand, I
return to the room.

"Maria," I interject, and she stops talking. "I brought you a
glass of wine."

She snatches the glass from me and takes a sip.

"I apologize, Maria, but I must return to my painting," Raphael
says, laying a hand on her arm. "Perhaps we can continue our
conversation another time."

In three quick swallows, Maria finishes her wine. She hands

me the glass without saying a word and gives Raphael a kiss on the lips. "Good-bye, my love."

She glides away, head held high. Her step falters. She regains her balance, smoothes and straightens her gown with her hands, and continues on, slower now, each step more arduous than the last. As the door closes, I catch a glorious glimpse of dread and puzzlement on her gorgeous face.

"Good-bye, Maria." I give Raphael's hand a squeeze. "Good-bye, forever."

Dear Dream Journal:
I looked up the word "orpiment" in Dad's dictionary. It's a deadly pigment made of arsenic. I killed her. I killed Diana.

I climb up to my top bunk, phone in hand, and get comfy. I've been waiting all day to talk to Di. I have to make sure she's still the same, still my best friend, and not mad at me. Ridiculous, but I can't help it.

The phone rings, as I'm about to call out. It's Di. I'm sure of it.

"Hi, it's me," she says.

"Hey, what a coincidence. I was just going to call you."

I wait for Di's voice to blare into my ear.

"Pen, I'm so mad!" she finally says.

I sit taller against the wall, frightened. "How come?"

"I pushed myself extra hard at dance class, because I

couldn't get the 'Rose Adagio' right," she says. "I got so frustrated, I almost bawled in front of everybody. And then, I snapped one of my pointe shoes and fell over. Now the only part of me that doesn't hurt is my nose."

What a relief. Nothing's wrong, other than her standard dance-meltdown.

"So, you're only upset about dance class. Everything else is okay?"

"Everything else is better than okay." Di's mood does an amazing one-eighty flip. "Did I tell you? I'm Aurora. You know, from *Sleeping Beauty*. I sleep for a hundred years and wait for my handsome prince to awaken me with a kiss."

"Well, don't pirouette near any spinning wheels, and you'll be fine."

Di laughs. "But the prince is really cute."

"What about Scott?" I ask. I'm afraid the time may have come for Di to chuck Scott in the trash with the other disposable guys.

"What about him?"

"Aren't you guys still going out?"

"I guess. He is fun to be around, but he's needy. Needy guys are annoying."

I don't know what to say to that, so I don't say anything at all. This time, it's disappointing to be right about Di dumping somebody. Luckily, she changes the subject.

When I get off the phone, I flip over and stare out my window. I can barely see the lake; it's a slightly lighter shade of black than the sky. That's my lake out there. And the Big

Dipper is out there, too. The night before I came here, Ryan explained to me why stars appear to twinkle and why we can see the Milky Way, even though we're in it. I wonder what he's doing at this very second while I'm staring at the sky.

A cricket chirps outside the window. He chirps again. How can such a tiny thing make such a huge racket? The little bugger will keep me up all night with his wing rubbing. I put on my headphones and press Play.

◆◆
◆ I slink into the shadows, watching Raphael and a woman make their drunken way down the narrow corridor of an inn. Fumbling like buffoons, they tussle with one of the doors, get it open, and fall inside, laughing wildly. The door slams.

Tiptoeing down the hall, I listen in on their too-loud conversation. He's complimenting her features and telling her how he'd love to paint her exquisite beauty. Tears come to my eyes when I hear him mumbling about a scandalous engagement he may have to end. I gaze down at the ruby ring on my left hand.

Then I overhear something else. And it isn't conversation. I listen for as long as I can bear, torturing myself, and then run down the stairs to the tavern. Is the woman upstairs my replacement, not only in Raphael's life, but in his paintings as well? I can't let that happen.

The barkeep strides across the room and backs me into a dimly lit corner, impossibly filling all space around me to prevent my escape. A cricket skitters out through a gap in his rotting sneer, then disappears into his nose.

"That woman upstairs. You intending to do her harm?" he

says, drawing closer. He ogles my hand. "I can help. For a price."

I whirl the ruby ring off my finger and reluctantly pass it to him. In his gnarled fingers, the ring becomes a small vial of yellow powder.

"Only the woman. You will not make a mistake?" I ask him, shrinking under his leering stare.

His silence does nothing to put my mind at ease. He slinks away.

Footsteps clomp down the stairs. I press flat against the wall and wait.

Raphael and the woman round the corner, together. They pass by, unaware that I'm watching them. Raphael's trembling hand unclenches, and a rose slowly glides through the air. The red petals fade to pink, then white, as their color seeps away like blood draining from a wound. At my feet, the rose hits the floor. White petals scatter, withered and lifeless.

I look up toward the door to cry out, but both Raphael and the woman are gone.

Dear Dream Journal:

This afternoon I did some research on Kate's computer while she was working in her darkroom. I learned that Raphael was so obsessed with his mistress Margherita (me) that he couldn't work away from her. She had to be brought along to stay with him so he could complete his jobs. Sweet, but slightly creepy. He was engaged to Maria (Diana) because she was the niece of his biggest patron, and he put off their wedding for six years. Before they could actually get married, Maria died. Surprise, surprise.

Raphael died suddenly, on his thirty-seventh birthday. Four months later, Margherita went to live with nuns in a convent for repentant women.

I wasn't sure what "repentant" meant, so I looked it up. It means feeling regret about having done something sinful.

13

Kate and I have been jogging together every night for almost two weeks. Trying to keep up with Kate has improved my jogging ability dramatically, and because she has so much to say, our jogs are never boring. Tonight we jogged for over an hour. I didn't let on that that's a big deal for me, but it is. I'm proud of myself.

In the short time we've known each other, we've become surprisingly good friends. Well, I guess it's not a big surprise to me since I sort of know Kate from my dreams, but under normal circumstances, our lightning-quick bond would be unusual. With most people, I'm reserved and I hold back a lot of stuff. Kate's such an easy and fun person to talk to, I feel like I could tell her anything.

And she wasn't kidding when she said she'd pester me about the ruby ring in the Raphael painting. Anything spherical or ruby-like sets her off. We've turned it into a game. Whenever I hear her say "Speaking of rings and rubies," I have three chances to guess the trigger object. We got lots of dirty looks in the grocery store yesterday when we couldn't stop laughing hysterically in the produce section. Their display of ruby red grapefruits was humungous.

Two hours ago, after our jog, Kate and I came down to Dad's beach. We haven't moved since. We're out of gas from running, but not tired enough to sleep. Sitting on the beach at night is relaxing, the perfect post-jog activity. I think Kate uses these quiet breaks to reload her brain, then she pulls a lever and everything spills out.

We talk about almost everything, and no subject is taboo. Kate's story about losing her virginity was so graphic I felt like I was right in the Wal-Mart stockroom with them.

There's a chunk of my life, though, that I've kept secret from everybody, including Kate. It's growing inside me. I'm becoming like one of those Jiffy Pop thingies, where the foil expands until it threatens to explode and shoot popcorn all over the kitchen. The foil holding back my secrets is stretched tight. And I'm beginning to smell smoke.

With a sharp knife, I poke a hole in the foil to let out some stream.

"Kate, don't you think it's strange that we ran into each other in roughly the same place almost every time we went running? How did you know when I was leaving?"

"Me? How did *I* know when *you* were leaving?" She laughs. "I was going to ask you the same thing. I've been running at about that same time, on that same route, since I was twelve. Then, all of a sudden, you showed up. And you kept showing up!" She laughs harder. "I was seriously starting to wonder if you were stalking me."

We laugh together, then put the conversation on hold while a couple holding hands strolls past us on the beach.

When they're out of earshot, I let out a little more steam.

"Kate, if I tell you something about me that's crazy, will you think I'm nuts?"

"I'm almost without a doubt, absolutely positive I won't think you're nuts."

I take a deep breath. "The day I came here, I had a dream that I was riding in a car. My dad's car." I bite my bottom lip, wondering if I should continue.

"This story better get a whole lot more interesting."

"It does. As I was riding along, the car changed, and I noticed a cigarette burn on the seat. The car in my dream was the same one my dad gave me when I got to his place. It even has the burn mark."

"Whoa, you're psychic. Now that is interesting."

I shake my head. "No, I'm not. There's no such thing as being psychic."

"Um, evidently there is, Psychic Penny."

Shaking my head again, I say, "I don't think so."

"Oh, I see. It was a big coincidence then. Is that what you're saying?"

Moonlight ripples across the surface of the lake. I stare across the water. "I don't know what to think."

We sit in silence for a while. I rest my chin on my bent knees. Kate's gaze annoyingly pokes at me. Poke, poke, poke.

"That's not the only time something like that happened to you, is it," she says.

My toes puncture the cool, damp sand. I scoop some up, tilt

my foot, and let the sand clumps fall. "You're right. It's not the only time."

"You can tell me, you know. I won't laugh. I'll think it's cool."

I grab a tiny flap of the shiny foil and pull. Popcorn spills all over the beach.

This morning, Kate showed up outside the patio door with a camera. She forced me to put way more effort into my appearance in one morning than I have all summer.

"Sit on that rock over there," Kate commands when we get to the beach.

I sit down and make a stupid face.

"Put your other face on," she says. "The one that's not scary."

My cheesy school-photo smile and stiff pose were banned within the first two seconds of this photo shoot. I'm supposed to act like myself.

Kate snaps a picture of me sitting sideways on the rock, hugging my drawn-up legs and staring off into space. Staring off into space—that's totally acting like myself.

"Excuse me, sir," Kate says, running over to an old man who's strolling down the beach. "Can you take a picture of my friend and me?"

He shrugs and takes the camera from Kate's hand. When we're arranged together, just how Kate wants us, she shouts a bunch of instructions. He looks at the camera like it's a VCR in need of digital clock programming, shrugs again, and snaps the photo.

Kate races over to rescue her precious camera from the clutches of Old Guy. "Thanks."

"Can I send a couple pictures to Ryan?" I ask when she gets back.

"Yeah, no problem. I'll make two sets and then we'll both have one."

Throughout the rest of the day, we travel around the town on foot, and finish up the roll of film in Kate's backyard.

"Want to stay for supper?" Kate asks, lowering her cell phone. "My mom says it's okay. The only catch is, it's my night to cook."

I take a break from typing an e-mail to Ryan on Kate's computer. "Sure. You're not making a reversible meal, are you?"

She snaps her fingers. "An excellent idea!" Into her phone, she says, "Penny's staying. We're making a special lasagna."

When she flips the phone shut, I say, "Where did the idea for reversibles come from?"

"I can't tell you. It's too weird," she says, mocking me.

"Har har."

"It all started because I'm a lefty. When I was a kid, I sometimes wrote words backwards, right to left, instead of left to right."

I try to picture that in my head. "You mean you could read them in a mirror?"

"Exactly. It's called mirror writing. When my dad got me

into art, I learned that Leonardo DaVinci wrote that way, too, so I started to mirror write on purpose. It made my diary too much of a pain in the ass for my mom to read."

"That's smart. I like it."

Kate shoves a blue-and-yellow pillow off her bed and takes a seat. "Things kind of took on a reversible life of their own from there."

I go back to typing my reply to the short e-mail Ryan sent a few days ago. Before I can finish, a new one arrives. The subject lines of his e-mails are usually silly one-liners. The latest one reads, *If a cow laughed, would milk come out her nose?*

The e-mail came with an attachment. I click on it as fast as I can, excited, like I'm unwrapping a present.

"Ryan sent me a picture from their fishing trip. Want to see what he looks like?"

She's already snooping from her bed, but she scoots to the end to get a better look.

Giving me a shove, she says, "Look at those eyes. He is hot!" She gets up and walks to the door. "I have to go to the grocery store. Want to come?"

"Sure. I'll be down in a minute, after I read the e-mail."

Hi Pen. Still swimming from 4-6 every day. The new guy (Legs) gave me a fly endurance workout. Kicks my butt. Tell Kate I made her protein powder fruit dip. Awesome. What else does she eat when she's training? Whey powder smoothies? I have a good recipe. She can really bench 130 lbs? Wow. Won't challenge her to arm-wrestle! Hey, check out the trout I caught at the cottage. TTYL. Ryan. (Miss you)

BTW, did you know that belly button lint is almost always blue?

I take one last, long look at Ryan and his fish. I miss him so much. I miss Di, and I even miss Mom. When I go home next month, I'll miss Sandy, and Dad, and Kate. Why can't all the people I care about be in my life at the same time?

◆
◆◆ Kate and I are running through the countryside. I feel
◆ good. Alive. I give Kate a quick smile. She smiles, too. The soft crunch of our feet hitting the ground is the only noise between us.

A raven suddenly speeds down through the air, as if hurtled from the sky, and splats on the road with a nauseating **thwunk**, its neck twisted at a severe angle. Kate and I cry out in surprise and disgust, skittering to a stop. Another blue-black bird strikes the road near my foot, and I slip on the gravel. Jagged pebbles stab my hands and arms.

A downpour of dead birds rains from the sky. Unable to dodge them, I tumble forward, falling and falling, through a dark cavernous space.

I emerge from the darkness into the starlit clearing, with Raven by my side. From an adjacent path, Diana and Leif also enter the clearing.

"Where's Erik?" Raven calls out.

Leif grips her shoulders. "He didn't make it out of the sea. He drowned."

Growing angry, Raven shakes her head in disbelief. "No, you're wrong."

"He was struggling and exhausted. But he refused to turn back." Leif sends me an accusatory glare. "He didn't want to risk losing."

This can't be happening. It wasn't supposed to end this way.

Diana and Leif grab hands at the edge of the cliff. Powerless, I watch their bodies fade from sight until there is nothing left where they stood.

"No!" I scream.

Twigs snap on the path. I spin around, surprised to see Ryan withdrawing into the forest. He shakes his head at me.

"What have you done, Astrid!" Raven whispers. "Erik was my brother. He loved you."

I try to get close to her, but she pushes me away.

Moving closer to the trees, she says, "I can't stay here."

"Don't go!" I cry, desperate. "I'll never see you again."

She retreats into the shadows and disappears.

"The stuff the psychic told you is coming true," Kate says as we're jogging past the beach playground. "So how come you wouldn't even consider that you might be psychic, too? You have proof, but you still don't believe."

I keep running full steam ahead.

"Very informative answer, Psychic Penny."

"I don't know why," I say, with more annoyance than I was aiming for. "This isn't a dream. It's my life. Maybe I don't want to accept that I might be psychic. I don't want to be different. Or crazy."

I suck in a deep breath, reminding myself never to talk that much while running again.

"You're okay with not having an explanation for what's happening to you?"

"Less talk, more breathe," I say, getting a cramp under my ribs.

Kate knows that I have lucid dreams, and I told her about the reading Margie gave me at Mom's party. I also told her about the fire drill coincidence during Ms. Watford's class, my inappropriate heckling of Louis during History class, and hear-

ing Leslie's thoughts inside my head. I didn't tell her what the
dreams were about or that I've had past-life dreams about her.
That would change our friendship too much, and not necessar-
ily for the better. I couldn't take the chance.

"All right, clam up, but I don't think you're crazy at all,"
Kate says. "What does your friend Diana think? Does she know
about your dreams and the millennium dude?"

"She does. But not much."

We run downhill. I take the chance to catch my breath.

"Bet you miss Di and Ryan. When are you going to go visit
them this summer?"

"I can't. They're hundreds of miles away."

"I know that. But I'm not expecting you to run there. Have
you forgotten what's sitting out in your dad's garage?"

"You think I should use my car?"

"No, I was thinking you'd fire up the old push broom he's
got out there."

I coast down the sloped street, able to laugh without
asphyxiating.

A visit to Di and Ryan is a great idea.

"Nope, not a good idea," Dad says, moving his head to peek
around me. I'm blocking the eleven o'clock news.

Remain calm. Save the tantrums for Mom.

"I'd only have to drive for a few hours, Dad. I'll go for a
weekend, that's it. I even know this great place where I can stay.
It's called My House."

Dad's not used to situations like this, where he has to take charge and think of ways to outsmart and outmaneuver me. He's the picture of befuddlement. "I don't like the idea of you driving that far by yourself," he says. "What if the car broke down?"

"What if I took Kate with me?" I shout, excited by my sudden ingenuity.

"I don't think your mother would like it if I let you drive on the highway."

"I'll call and ask."

On to the next round of questions—Dad quizzes me on everything his whirring brain can think up on short notice. Do you know how to pump gas? Can you change a tire? Do you have enough money? Do you pick up hitchhikers?

My answers to the questions aren't well thought out, but they're good. I'm wearing Dad down. I can see it in his glazed-over eyes.

"Call your mom in the morning," Dad says, and I hold back a triumphant whoop. "If it's okay with her and Kate's allowed to go with you, I'll let you go for the weekend."

"Thanks, Dad. You're the best!" *Did my mouth just say that?*

It's trip day. I met all of Dad's criteria; he had to let me go. I told Mom to keep our visit secret. Everybody's going to be so surprised to see us.

I hear a tapping noise on the patio door. I whirl around and run over to let Kate in. "I said I'd pick you up at noon," I cry, feeling guilty that she walked all the way over here carrying her luggage.

The bags drop to the kitchen floor, and she stretches her arms. "I couldn't wait any longer. And I'm used to coming over at this time anyway." She unzips one of the bags and pulls out a manila envelope. "I brought your set of photos."

I take the envelope from her hand and open it on our way to the kitchen table. "I hope I don't look too stupid," I say, carefully sliding the stack of pictures out.

The first picture is of me. I think. The girl in the black-and-white photo is beautiful.

"Do you have a magic darkroom, Kate? Look at me in this photo."

I lay it on the table and move on to the next picture, the one of me sitting on the rock at the beach, hugging my legs. Wispy strands of hair flutter back from my profile as I gaze off into space.

Slowly, I go through all the pictures. Each one is incredible, especially the nature shots I'm absent from. When I get to the final photo in the stack, my hand flies up to my throat, but it's unable to hold back a gasp. The photo is the one Old Guy took of Kate and me. Close-ups of our faces are centered and in focus, then the beach background gradually fuzzes out.

"That's called a vignette," Kate says. "Do you like it?"

Not wanting Kate to know I'm choked up, I lean closer to the black-and-white picture, pretending to get a better look. It takes all my concentration to calmly say, "I love it. It's the best photo I've ever seen."

"Let's go," Kate says, leaving the table. "And don't forget your running shoes."

I gently insert the pictures into the envelope, with the photo of Raven and Astrid, together again, at the very top of the stack.

Saying good-bye to Sandy wasn't fun. She knew I was leaving, and I felt awful. As we were pulling away, I saw her furry face pressed against the patio door. What will I do when I have to go home for real? I can't call a dog on the phone to chat. Or can I?

Even Kalli was sad that I was leaving. She straggled out of bed to give me a dejected "See ya later." She had the chance to come with us—Dad's idea, not mine—but she didn't want to leave her new best friend, Little Miss Annoying. I called Dad at work before we left to say good-bye, which led to another round of testing. Seems he'd remembered more worst-case possibilities. By the time we got out of the house, put gas in the car, backtracked to an ATM, and grabbed some takeout at Wendy's, it was pushing three o'clock.

"When I talked to Ryan the other night, I almost blabbed about our visit, but I caught myself in time."

"Did you talk to Diana?"

"No. I called but she was out doing something with wonder-twins Rick and Emma."

"Pass this loser," Kate says, pointing a fry at the car ahead of us. "He's a hat-driver."

"I can't, I don't like to pass when I'm driving. And what's a hat-driver?"

"Anybody who wears a hat while driving drives *veeery* slow-ly. It's a universal law."

I crawl along behind the hat-driver until I'm wishing I could ramp onto his car and crush him into a hat-wearing pancake.

"All right, I'll pass him," I say. "I'm two minutes away from an aneurysm."

I check every mirror a dozen times, and pull out to pass when the other lane is clear for as far as I can see. The steering wheel vibrates in my hands. When I'm safely past the hat-driver, I pull back into my lane and exhale the breath I was holding.

Kate noisily slurps up every last drop of her Coke. She lets out a satisfied *aaaahh*, and says, "Are we there yet?"

I'm waiting at a busy intersection in a city about twenty minutes from home. This is the longest red light in history. I tap my fingers on the steering wheel, eager to get going. It's only six o'clock, but it's getting dark. Rain clouds are billowing up in the sky, and I don't like to drive when it's dark or when it's raining.

A city bus rolls into the middle of the intersection to make a left turn onto the street I'm on. The interior of the bus is aglow, making the rectangular windows look like movie screens. My gaze stops on a man seated alone, wearing a red shirt. The invisible feathers lightly roll down my bare arms.

Something bad is going to happen to him.

A drawn-out horn blast from the car behind me makes me jump.

"Pen, the light isn't going to get any greener."

I snap back to paying attention and accelerate through the intersection.

"Something the matter?" Kate asks. "You look freaked out."

"It's nothing," I say, but the horrible feeling that came over me when I saw the man is clinging to me like plastic wrap.

I follow the bus, separated by a few cars. At the next street, the bus turns into a mall parking lot. As I drive past, I glance out my window, catching a glimpse of the red shirt. My gut takes over, and I impulsively swerve into the next turning lane.

"Hey, are we going to the mall?" Kate says. "I forgot to pack my deodorant."

Only half-listening, I say, "Yeah, sure."

I drive through the lot and pull into a spot near the bus. The man is nowhere in sight.

"Aren't you coming?" Kate asks, when I make no move to get out of the car.

It hits me that I'm acting strangely, for no good reason. I shut off the ignition. "Sorry, I'm just spaced out."

We wait for traffic to clear the thoroughfare, and walk to the closest entrance.

"There's a drugstore," Kate says, veering to the left. I have to jog next to her to keep up with her super-athletic walk. Four guys hanging out at the ATM check Kate out, but she strides past, oblivious. "We should get sports drinks. In case we run tonight."

Inside the store, I browse around while Kate inspects rows and rows of deodorants. I grab a magazine, some gum, and two sports drinks. Rounding the end of the aisle, I freeze. The man in the red shirt is standing in the pick-up line at the pharmacy counter. I hurry back the way I came and meet up with Kate at the checkout.

"You're getting deodorant for men?" I say, peering into her handcart.

"I like the way guys smell. Why would I want to walk around smelling like a girl?"

The old man in line ahead of us is arguing with the cashier over a five-cent difference between the weekly flyer price and the price he was charged. I don't envy her one bit.

Eventually, it's our turn. I'm all business at the counter. No phony small talk, no fuss. We're out of the store in no time. We push the heavy mall doors open and leave the air conditioning behind. The air is so thick I could drink it through a straw.

And then I see the man in the red shirt. Again.

Kate points him out, as he walks through the parking lot. "That guy dropped his wallet. I should run it to him." Over her shoulder, she says, "Meet you at the car."

Kate jogs away, zigzagging between three concrete planters, and waits for a car at the nearby stop sign to pass. The driver leans over the steering wheel, staring at the road. She must see the wallet, because she stops to let Kate go ahead and rescue it.

I'm glad Kate decided to return the wallet. I saw the man drop it, too, but I was going to ignore it. I didn't come to this mall to get deodorant, or a magazine, or anything else. I came because I followed the man in the red shirt here. And now he keeps getting thrown in my path. I should have kept driving, like a normal person would have. But I keep thinking about the other time a strange, unexpected thought popped into my head. Right before the fire alarm went off in Ms. Watford's class.

On the way to my car, I spy on Kate and the man. He stops and pats down his pockets. The patting gets more frantic. He spins around and starts to jog back. Kate waves the wallet in the air. Even from where I'm standing, I can see the relief in his face.

I start the car, roll down the windows, and reverse out of the parking spot. In my side mirror, I watch Kate talk to the man. She waves. He waves. She runs to the car, smiling.

"There's my good deed for the day," Kate says, bouncing onto her seat. "Now I get to be bad to balance everything out."

At the thoroughfare, I look left and right a few times, not sure how I got into this mall.

"Wait, don't go yet." Kate presses on my arm, as if that'll hold the whole car back.

A beat-up black pickup blasts straight through the stop sign. It whizzes past the front of my car, going faster than I'm comfortable driving on the highway. The driver is too busy reaching into the glove compartment to look at the road.

Kate's reaction time is way better than mine. Swearing, she springs up and sticks her head out her window, before I have a chance to say anything. By now, the speeding truck is squealing out of the parking lot, but Kate hollers, "Go a little faster why don't ya! Jerk!"

With the truck already out of sight, the only other person in

Kate's line of fire is the old man who was arguing with the cashier in the drugstore. He shuffles across the road, scowling and grumbling under his breath.

"Let's get out of here." Kate drops down, laughing hysterically. "Looks like he's about to throw his Metamucil at us."

We leave the mall and get back on the road to my house. The sticky horrible feeling I got when I came here stays behind.

Singing along with Kate and the radio makes the rest of the trip fly by. We crest a hill and then my city comes into view, a sea of lights in the distance. A tingling zap shoots across my chest when we cruise past the first few houses at the city limits. *Brockton: Population 75,000. Ambitious Present, Bright Future.*

"Let's go straight to Di's house," I say, cruising past my place.

I pull into their driveway and park, so excited I nearly rear-end their car. We run up the porch steps, and I press the doorbell. Faint chimes float out through the door, and then Di's schnauzer, Misty, announces our arrival with frenzied barking. Through the frosted glass inset in the door, I see a tall, blurry shape with broad shoulders strolling down the hall. I can barely breathe. Kate and I exchange gritted-teeth smiles.

The door swings open.

My stomach rises in my gut, like I'm whooshing down a steep roller coaster. I was expecting Di's dad to open the door. Not *him.*

"Penny, it's you."

"Hi, is Diana here?" My voice sounds hollow and far away.

I stare at the doorbell that gave away my arrival. It's too late to back down the steps and run away.

"She's downstairs, watching a movie. C'mon in, and I'll get her."

"Omigod! Penny!" Di screams from somewhere inside the house.

Next thing I know, Di's dragging us inside, Misty is jumping all over me, scratching my bare legs with her serrated schnauzer claws, and there's too much squealing and barking and hugging going on. Then, as if that wasn't enough, the phone starts ringing. "The cordless is in my room," Di calls over her shoulder.

When I manage to get loose from our group hug, the three of us are standing alone in the front hallway.

Kate gives a hasty wave. "Hi, I'm Kate."

"Kate! I've heard so much about you."

Di leads us into the kitchen. I trail behind on stiff legs, my brain relaying conflicting messages to my body.

"So, who was the stud who answered the door?" Kate asks, and I want to melt into a puddle on the hardwood floor.

"That was Rick."

"Rick? His name is Rick?" I ask, leaning against a kitchen chair.

"Yeah, remember, I told you about him over the phone. Lots of times."

"He knew who I was when he opened the door."

Di points to my eleventh-grade picture prominently displayed on the fridge. "Of course he knew who you were. I talk about you so much he probably feels like he already knows you."

"Oh, right."

Rick walks into the kitchen and sets the phone on the counter. "It was your mom. They'll be home around ten." He crosses the room, saying, "Can you guys stay? I'll go restart the movie."

We are not staying here, that's all there is to it. I open my mouth to tell him that we have to get going to my place, my mom's waiting.

"A movie. Sounds good, we're into that," Kate says, and I clench the chair.

"Great." Rick jogs downstairs to the family room.

My gaze darts around the kitchen and settles on the phone. There's one person I need to talk to. Now. "Di, I'm gonna call Ryan. Can he come over, too?"

Di's smile droops. "Ryan's not home. You didn't know that?"

"What do you mean? Where is he?"

"I ran into him last night at the mall. He said he and his dad were taking Scott on a canoe trip or something." Di shakes her head and her tiny ballet slipper earrings twirl. "I dunno. I wasn't really listening. There was this phenomenal purple sweater in the front window of Clothes Horse."

Kate turns to look at me, one eyebrow cocked higher than the other.

"I'm sorry," Di says. "But you'll get to see him in, what, two weeks, right?"

Pretending to be engrossed in the newspaper laid out on the table, I say, "Yeah."

"You guys want Cokes for the movie?" The fridge door opens.

"I do," Kate says, at the same time I say, "Sure."

Di sets two cans on the table. "Let's go. I'll introduce you to Emma."

Kate starts to follow behind Di. I tug on her shirt, hoping she'll get the hint.

"We'll be down in a minute," Kate says. "I had to go pee the whole way here, but Penny refused to pull over. That's fairly evil, if you ask me."

Di laughs on her way out of the room.

"Okay, what's up?" Kate whispers. When I look up from the newspaper, her features go into reverse, as if I'm a monster they must retreat from at warp speed. "You've got a bunch of red splotches all over your face like you're ready to kaboom." Her hands fly out next to her face, mimicking an explosion. "Are you upset that Ryan's not home?"

I pat tears away with my sleeve. "Yeah, that."

"You humans and your faulty eyes," Kate says with a sly grin.

"And Rick's the guy."

"The *what* guy?" Her eyes go wide. "*That* guy?"

"Yes." I exhale.

"I thought you said his name had to start with *U*. And he doesn't look like a lion."

Rubbing my temples, I squint my eyes shut. "I don't understand. Margie said I'd know him when I saw him. And I know Rick is the guy."

"You're sure?"

When Rick opened the door, my mind took a snapshot of him—blond, tall, and handsome in a majestic kind of way. From that, I got an overwhelming feeling, the kind of feeling I've been waiting for since Mom's party.

"I'm positive." I try to conjure up the snapshot image. "He is. I think."

"I'm sensing some doubt, with a touch of delusion sprinkled on top."

I give Kate a squint-eyed glare.

"All right, if you say he's the guy, then he's the guy."

"What do I do now?"

"You're going to go downstairs to watch a movie with your best friend, Diana, and her new friends, Rick and Emma, that's what you're going to do."

"But," I start to protest, and Kate does one of her emphatic hand swishes at me.

"You can do this. Now let's go."

Rick must think I hate him. We've been watching movies and listening to music for hours, and I haven't made eye contact with him or spoken to him once. I keep my focus firmly entrenched on Emma, Diana, Kate, the floor, the TV, the chair I'm sitting on, and my lap. I still don't have a clear-cut image of what Rick looks like.

"Hello, down there," Di's mom calls down the stairs. "Time to wrap up the party, Diana, your dad and I are going to bed."

"Yeah, yeah," Di says.

Rick and Emma stand. "It was nice to meet you, Kate and Penny," Rick says, and Emma chimes in with, "We'll see you tomorrow."

I smile at Emma. "It was great to meet you guys, too."

"Maybe we can all go out someplace tomorrow," Kate helpfully suggests.

"Sounds good," Rick says. He leans over Di, and she boosts herself off the couch.

Rick is well within my field of vision. I'm supposed to look away, but I can't. Their lips meet in a kiss that declares they're way beyond the "just friends" stage of the game.

My heart cracks. Straight down the middle.

15

Kate and Di are sound asleep on my bedroom floor. I'm sitting in bed, huddled over my dream journal in near darkness, jotting down my latest dream before I forget it.

Dear Dream Journal:

I was in a field, surrounded by sheep. Malcolm walked over in his kilt and I gave him a kiss. Gross black lumps bubbled up all over his body. Di walked into the field, so I ran to her to get help. In a thick Scottish accent, she started shouting something about Malcolm being her husband, and I had no right. She yanked a handful of wildflowers out of the ground and beat me over the head with them, screaming that I never should have come to her farm, that I should go back where I came from. Then the black lumps popped up all over her, too. The flowers in her hand wilted into black ash. Giving me a dead stare, she said, "We all fall down."

Kate rolls over in her sleeping bag and tugs the zipper open. Without noticing me, she crawls out, staggers to standing, and heads toward the bathroom.

"Hey," I whisper.

She spins around in a karate-chop pose. "You scared the hell out of me. What are you doing awake right now?"

"I'm writing a dream in my journal." I lean over and peek at Di's face to make sure she's still asleep. "I think we should go home."

"What for? We just got here. And besides, you are home."

"I know, but I have a bad feeling about being here now. I think we should leave."

"We're only staying for two days, Pen. Don't worry about it." She takes a seat on the bed next to me. "Sorry, I know you think Rick is the same person you've been in love with for a thousand years. It must have freaked you out to see him."

"That's an understatement."

"He might not feel like a stranger to you," she says, "but you are a stranger to him."

The truth hurts. In my dreams, I've felt the most intense love for a person who has no idea who I am. He has no knowledge of any of it. I'm the one who's burdened with all those feelings, all the experiences from the past.

"What are you planning to do, now that you know who Rick is? Stake a claim on him and take him away from your best friend? I haven't known you long, but I know you wouldn't do anything to make Di unhappy. You have to accept that he's her boyfriend."

I stare at the dream journal in my lap. I didn't understand what was happening before, but things are even foggier now. My brain hangs out a *Do Not Disturb* sign.

After using the bathroom, Kate gives me a reassuring smile and crawls back into her sleeping bag. Within minutes, she's conked out again.

Exhausted, I tilt my head back and rest it on the headboard. I won't go to sleep; I have too many things to make sense of. I'll just rest my eyes . . .

◆◆ I'm sitting in the school cafeteria across the table from
◆ Valerie. If anybody can help me with my lucid-dream problem, it's Val.

She slaps a spiral notebook on the table between us, the typewritten word **Script** the only thing on the cover. "I think dreams are a way for our brains to tell us things we don't or can't normally think about. What are your nightmares trying to tell you?"

"That I've been in love with the same person for a thousand years."

Val's eyebrows lift, questioning my answer.

"What! That's what they're about. He's been in each of my past lives."

Val shakes her head. "I'm disappointed in you, Penny. You're not thinking hard enough. I was sure you'd use this opportunity wisely."

What is Val talking about? What opportunity! I think now's a good time to wake myself up from this dream.

"You wrote the answers," Val says. "But did you read them!"

She flips her notebook open. On the first page is the word **Rewrite.**

It's a gorgeous morning, but I'm too wound up to enjoy it. All my muscles are tensed, and a troop of pimples decided to make camp on my face sometime during the night. A pretty picture I am not.

We're on our way to have a picnic in a huge nature park near Rick and Emma's old town. Kate keeps taking off her seat belt to turn around and join the backseat rowdiness. I hate when people don't wear seat belts. Don't they realize I'm trying to drive?

For the hundredth time, Kate leans over the back of her seat, this time to share her insights on whether or not Bigfoot is real. Personally, I'm not sure about Bigfoot, but I can testify that Big*mouth* is no mythical creature. It's taking all my strength to keep from smacking her butt as it waggles around beside me.

A shrill laugh from Emma sends a major déjà vu vibe through me, and my hands squeeze the steering wheel. I knew she was going to do that.

Plopping down in her seat, Kate says, "Rick, you're crazy."

This announcement sets off a debate that sounds eerily familiar, as if I'm listening to a recording of a conversation they've already had. And it's not a conversation I want to hear twice. I try to tune them out.

Turn right at the fruit stand, I think, taking my foot off the gas pedal.

Di taps me on the shoulder. "Pen, make a right turn at the roadside fruit stand."

I turn onto a bumpy gravel road. A shiver goes down my back as we shimmy past the fruit stand, and I take a deep breath, hoping this strange déjà vu feeling will go away. Thankfully, it does. The conversation bouncing around the car quickly loses all familiarity, and Emma's shrieks bore through my skull with no warning at all. I drive down the winding road, find the park on my own, with no help from the chatty bunch, and pull into the empty parking lot near the hiking trails.

All I heard this morning was nature park this, nature park that. If this place is so damn great, why are we the only people here?

We grab the backpacks from the trunk.

"We'll lead the way," Di says, smiling at Rick. "We've been here lots of times."

What's that mean? Is this their favorite get-busy locale? Ewwww.

Holding hands, Di and Rick take the lead and march us into the woods. Surprisingly, the forest isn't dense and dark like I was expecting. It's airy, colorful, and full of sunlight. Bright wildflowers line the trail and the forest floor beyond is green with plants. A chipmunk darts across the path in front of us, a fuzzy ball of speed.

"Too bad I didn't bring my camera," Kate says to me. "I'd get some great shots here."

"Definitely." I smile at Kate and go back to watching Di and Rick hold hands.

Just when I'm working up a good sweat, Di and Rick take a detour and lead us into the woods down a small path that's barely visible. Branches slap my legs and scratch my arms. After a few minutes, the trail opens into a secluded clearing by a lake.

"Whoa, it's beautiful here," Kate says. "Look how sparkly the water is."

Di smiles proudly. "This is our secret spot. We found it ourselves."

The lake is puny, nothing like my lake at Dad's. There isn't even a sand beach.

"It's great, Di," I say.

"I knew you guys would like it."

Rick drops his backpack and pulls out a folded blanket.

"Shit," Rick says, rifling through the backpack. "I forgot my inhaler at home."

"Yeah, I saw it in the bathroom," Emma says.

"Why didn't you tell me?"

She pulls a cellophane-wrapped sandwich from her bag. "I assumed you'd grab it."

"Look at all the trees and pollen and dust around me. It's hot and I'm hiking," he says, jumping to his feet. "What if I have an asthma attack out here? I could die, Emma. You know that."

Not even flinching, Emma says, "Don't flip out on me because you forgot something."

Di scrambles to her feet. "It's okay, don't worry," she says, soothingly, like a mom would. She grabs his hand. "I'm sure

Pen will let us borrow her car, we'll drive back into town, get the inhaler, and be back here in no time."

I'm not sure about the "no time" part of that sentence. It took half an hour to drive out here. "No problem," I say. I unzip the front pouch of my backpack and fish out the car keys. I'm too afraid to walk over and hand them to Rick. Instead, I toss them to him. Unfortunately, I throw with the skill of an infant. The keys zing through the air and miss his outstretched hand. If I'd been aiming for his crotch, I'd have hit a bull's-eye.

Rick bends at the waist to grab the keys from the ground, saying, "Ooooph," but he's laughing at the same time. I couldn't be any more mortified.

"Hey, since you're going back into town," Emma says, "could you grab my towel? I forgot it in the bathroom. And buy a couple of bags of chips while you're out."

Ignoring his sister, Rick turns to face me. "Thanks for letting us use your car, Penny. I really appreciate it."

"No problem," I say, giving a warm smile to the picnic blanket.

I hear branches cracking and evergreen bows rustling. Assuming that Rick and Di have left, I look up. Rick's gone, but Di's walking over to me. She squats beside the blanket. "Pen, you've been acting different since you got here. You don't have to be shy around Rick and Emma, okay? They're great. They'll like you no matter what."

Di thinks I'm acting strangely out of shyness. Should I tell her the real reason?

I haven't known you long, but I know you wouldn't do anything to make Di unhappy, Kate whispers inside my head.

"Di, I just pegged him in the nuts."

"Don't worry about that, either." On her way to the path, Di turns around. "Bye, guys, see you in an hour." She disappears into the brush.

"What do you do when you come out here, Emma?" Kate asks.

"Well, I smoke lots of weed and lie on a rock near the lake." Emma pulls a plastic Baggie from her backpack. "I'm heading down to the rock. Are you guys coming?"

"That's okay," I say. Thank goodness, I stuck my journal in the backpack before we left. I pull it out and hold it up for Emma to see. "I'll stay here and write for a while."

"And I'll stay here and watch her write," Kate says. As Emma's leaving the clearing, Kate shouts, "Hey, Emma, does your brother's name start with *U*?"

"Yeah, it's Ulrich, but don't tell him I told you. He'd kill me."

Kate turns to look at me. I've never seen anybody's eyes nearly pop out of their sockets. Until now. "By any chance, is he a lion?" she asks.

I expect that question to elicit a funny look from Emma. But it doesn't even faze her.

"He was, before we moved. He played soccer for the East-lawn Lions."

"He plays soccer with bad asthma?" I ask.

"He does all kinds of sports. His asthma's not that bad, he's just a big baby about his inhaler," she says, strolling toward the lake. "I've only seen him almost die twice."

And the winner of the Sweetest Sister in the World is.

"He played for the Lions?" Kate whispers to me. "Think that's what the psychic meant?" Before I have the chance to answer, she calls out, "When's Rick's birthday?"

"August fifth." The trees close around Emma. "We had his party last week!"

"That makes him a Leo, like my mom," I say. "He's a lion in more ways than one."

Kate slaps her thigh. "Okay, I lied about believing you before. But I definitely believe you now. He's the guy all right."

"Told you so." I know Rick is the guy, but to hear Margie's reading confirmed by Emma freaks me out.

Kate grabs my journal. It flaps open and my pen falls out. "So, what are we writing?"

"Nothing," I say, grabbing it out of her hands. "I think I'm supposed to figure out the dreams that are already in my journal."

"You mean, take the important parts and organize them into an easy-to-read and informative list? I'll help you alphabetize."

"Kate, you're a genius!"

"That's what they've been trying to tell me for years."

I wanted to keep my dreams secret, but I'd be stupid not to let someone as smart as Kate help me figure them out. "I'm going to let you read my journal."

"Excellent," she says, rubbing her hands together.

I open the book to the first entry. "In the first few dreams, I was Marie Antoinette."

Kate's lips sputter and she falls over backward, screaming with laughter.

"Are you gonna help or not?"

She gets ahold of herself and sits up. "Yes, your majesty."

"Listen, Kate," I say in a stern teacher voice. "You must take this seriously. If you can't behave, I'll send you to the rock to get stoned with Emma."

Kate hangs her head sheepishly. "I'll be good."

I hand off the journal, already wincing in embarrassment.

Her eyeballs zigzag as she speed-reads. "Vikings. Cool," she drawls. Finger-lick and flip. "Penny, you poison-wielding femme fatale, you." She goes back to reading. "Ahhh, the Plague. What a way to go."

"The Plague? Who had the Plague?"

"Malcolm. Hence the black lumps and the ring-around-the-rosy reference. We're talking Symbolism for Beginners, here."

I take a swing at her head, but she weaves out of the way, chuckling.

When she finally sets the book on her lap, I say, "So what did you get from all that?"

Kate takes a deep breath, and a look of complete seriousness wipes the joking and fun right out of her face. "You didn't tell me that Di and the millennium guy died every time. Hasn't that set off any alarm bells in your head?"

My mind whirrs, burrowing out a memory. I think I said

something strange to Ryan at the end-of-school party, when I was drunk, and he had no clue what I was talking about. What did I say? It's on the tip of my brain.

. . . *She's died a horrible, violent death . . . I always feel so guilty . . . like it's my fault.*

"I also noticed," Kate pauses, "that in almost every life Di likes the millennium guy."

"Huh?"

She flips the book open. "Let's see. Di's engaged to him when he's Raphael. Di's married to him when he's Malcolm. They committed suicide to spend eternity with each other." Staring me straight in the eye, she says, "Did you ever consider that maybe Di's the one who's meant for him . . . and not you?"

"Omigod." I shake my head. "Then I come along and everything gets screwed up?"

Kate shrugs sympathetically and flips through the journal entries. "Okay, I get who you, Di, and Rick are in the dreams. But who's Raven?"

She stares at me while I struggle to come up with an answer. I don't want to lie to her.

My voice jumps all over the place, but I get an answer out. "You're gonna think I'm too insane to be friends with anymore, but Raven is you, Kate."

"Whoa," she says.

I can't gauge her reaction by her expression, I'm too afraid to look at her face, but judging by her deep "whoa," I'd say she's astounded.

"Raven is me? For real? I was in your Viking dreams?"

I nervously glance at her face and nod.

"Well, if that isn't the coolest thing ever, I don't know what is!" she says, and my tensed cheeks relax. "Boy, the gang's all here—me, you, Di, and Rick. You should have told me I was coming to our thousand-year reunion!"

Kate laughs and starts to say something, but I cut her off, suddenly anxious about the comment she made about us all being together again.

"Wait, I just remembered two dreams that I didn't write about. You know about the car dream I had on the way to Dad's house, but I only told you part of it. My car was on fire. Di turned to look at me, and her face was dead and rotting. She told me I had to leave to get away from her. And in the other dream, a friend told me I'm not using the opportunity I've been given, wisely. What opportunity?"

"I don't know. Your psychic powers?"

I sit rigid on the blanket and stare at the towering evergreen tree over Kate's shoulder until it melds into a fuzzy green blob. All this time, I've been concerned with the weirdness of having the past-life dreams and the visions. I was so wrapped up in me, me, me, and how strange my life had become, that I never stopped to think about why those things were happening to me. If I've been screwing up for the last thousand years, maybe this is my chance to fix things. Maybe I've been given an amazing opportunity.

"Val also showed me a book with the words *Script* and *Rewrite* on it."

"Rewrite script?" Kate says. "What's that mean?"

I swallow hard, feeling queasy. *What if the script says I'm supposed to tie my shoe, but I decide against it? The whole movie would have to be rewritten from that point on.*

"It means I shouldn't tie my shoe this time," I whisper, staring at the smudgy evergreen tree.

"Um, Pen? Didn't you say your car was on fire? And Diana was dead?"

Kate continues on, but her words blur like the tree. Invisible fingers creep up the back of my neck. Against the green screen, I see a road stretched out ahead of me. I'm high above the road, as if I'm sitting in a truck. In the distance, a car speeds down the road toward me. My view of the road shudders violently, as I swerve into the other lane. The car is closer now. It's my car. I can't move or look away. I can only watch the road. The car approaches the fruit stand. The sound of tearing and grinding metal peels through my head. Fire flares up before my eyes. The fruit stand blows apart.

"Penny, are you okay?" Kate's shaking me. Urgently. "What's wrong?"

I look at her, feeling drowsy like I've just woken up. My shoulders lurch forward. On hands and knees, I scramble to the edge of the blanket to throw up onto the grass.

"What's wrong?" Kate cries.

With the corner of the blanket, I wipe off my mouth. "I just saw Di and Rick get in a car accident on their way back, near the fruit stand. I came here and now they're going to die. Again." My stomach compresses and I barf all over the blanket this time.

Kate paces around in front of me. "How much time do we have?"

I glance at my watch. "About half an hour."

"We have half an hour," Kate says. "And we're stuck in the middle of nowhere."

 "We can't sit here and
do nothing. Get up, Pen. Let's think."

I hold up my hand and dry-heave.

Kate grabs my hand and pulls me to standing. "We don't
have time for you to barf your ass off now. Let's move!"
Dragging me by the bottom of my T-shirt, she leads me to the
flat rock where Emma is stretched out in the sun. "Emma, get
up. We need help."

Emma shields her bloodshot eyes with one hand. "What do
you need help with?"

"Do you have a cell phone?"

"Yes," she says.

"Give it to us!" I cry.

"It's not here, silly, it's at home. It doesn't get a signal here
anyway."

Kate's bellowed obscenities echo back to us. "Emma, we
need to get to the fruit stand in half an hour. Is there any way
we can get a boat, a plane, a car? Anything?"

"You want some fruit?" Emma drawls. "I think I've got an
apple in my backpack. If I do, can you grab it for me?"

"She's stoned out of her mind, Kate. She's never gonna be able to help us."

With the force of two men, Kate reaches down, grabs Emma's arm, and pulls her to standing. "What's the quickest way to get to the goddamned fruit stand?"

Emma points to the lake.

"What?" I squeal. "What's that mean?"

Swatting at invisible flying insects, Emma says, "The road goes all the way around the lake. That takes a long time." She points to the lake again. "The fruit stand is on the other side of the lake, right over there, straight across, like an arrow."

Kate and I turn to each other, letting Emma mumble to herself.

"How long do you figure it would take us to swim across?" I ask.

Kate studies the lake. "A long time."

"Think it will be hard?"

"Does it matter?"

We step off the rock, fully clothed and wearing our shoes, onto the slippery bottom of the lake and wade into the water until it's waist deep. Together, we plunge in and start the front crawl. Right away, I'm struggling for breath. I flip onto my back, but Kate powers on. I take a deep breath, flip over, and go back to sprint swimming. Water splashes into my mouth. Swallowing and sputtering, I switch to a sidestroke and breathe through my nose to hold back a choking fit. Kate pulls ahead, kicking up big waves that swell over my head and threaten to drown me. Back in a front crawl, I kick hard to catch up. My thighs burn. Finally, on one of my breaths, I lift my head, and the opposite shore of the lake is right in front of us.

"I can touch bottom," I gasp, starting the run to the shore.

We practically crawl out of the lake, wringing water out of our T-shirts.

"How much time do we have?" Kate asks as we run down the gravel road that leads to the fruit stand.

"Five minutes."

Our arms and legs pump. My body taps into energy reserves I didn't even know I had. We can do this. I know we can.

Gravel rolls beneath my shoes like marbles, and my feet skitter out from beneath me. I flip backwards, landing flat on my butt. Sharp pebbles shred the skin on my hands and arms. I cry out, more from anger than pain.

Kate keeps running, gaining a big lead in a matter of seconds. "Get up, Penny!" she screams. "Keep going!"

Ignoring the pain and the blood trickling down my arm, I stagger a few steps and then get back into a sprint. Just as I'm catching up to Kate, the roof of the fruit stand comes into view above the trees that line the road. We're almost there.

"Run harder," Kate commands.

I can't tell Kate that I'm running as hard as I can. That would require oxygen. I'm breathing as quickly and shallowly as I can without dying. My watch says we have about one minute left. The seconds tick away in my pounding head. I estimate there are a hundred footfalls, at least, before we reach the fruit stand.

At fifty footfalls, long stretches of the paved road are visible in both directions. I look to the left and spot my car, far off in the distance. Looking to the right, I see the truck. And not just any truck; it's an eighteen-wheeler. Both vehicles are about equal distances away from us.

"Let's go!" I shout, and we race toward the intersection.

"Go to your car. Motion for them to pull over!"

At the intersection, we make a sharp left and sprint down the side of the road, waving our arms in the air. My car speeds toward us.

Exaggeratedly pointing to my left, I motion for Rick and Di to pull off the road. Beside me, Kate does the same. But the car keeps on coming.

The road hums beneath my feet. I can hear the truck barreling down on us.

"Pull off the road!" Kate shrieks.

We persist with our arm signals. As our running bodies align with the fruit stand, my car skids, fishtailing onto the side of the road. Huge clouds of dust fill the air.

"Truck!" I hear Kate holler over a deafening rumble.

The suction of the truck careening off the road behind us nearly stops me in my tracks. Ferocious wind whips my hair around my head, blinding me. I run on in the same forward direction.

Wood cracks and shatters as the fruit stand is hit.

"This way!" Rick is shouting.

A large object zings past my head, nearly sending me into a face-first dive to the pavement. Someone wraps their arms around me and hurries me away. I want to keep running, but I'm pulled back. Disoriented, I stop and push my hair back from my eyes.

Rick grabs my arms and forces me to look him in the face. "Penny, are you okay?"

Am I okay? I don't know. Without warning, my legs give out. Rick catches me as I fall forward.

"I don't know what to say, Penny," he whispers in my ear, his voice choked with emotion. "I think you and Kate just saved our lives."

"There must be something really wrong with the driver of that truck," Rick says, physically vibrating next to me at the side of the road.

Kate takes off running, through the shallow ditch beside the road and across the field, heading straight for the truck.

"You guys stay here." Rick's hands clench and unclench. "I'll go call for help."

Di opens the passenger-side door of my car and sits sideways on the seat with her legs hanging out of the car. "That was so close." She puts her face in her hands. "If you guys hadn't been there . . ."

Over my shoulder, I look at the truck. I can't see Kate anywhere.

"Di, I'm going to see if Kate needs help."

"No, stay here," she says, wiping her eyes.

I look at the truck again. No sign of Kate or the truck driver. Pain rips through my legs when I squat in front of Di. "I have to go see if she needs help. Rick will be right back. You have to stay here for when help comes."

I go to stand and catch a glimpse of myself in the side-view mirror. My hair is plastered to my cherry-red face, caked with dirt and sweat. I lick beads of dusty saltwater off my upper lip. All the muscles in my legs are stiffening up, bad, and after a near wipeout in the ditch, I jog across the field, glancing at the demolished fruit stand on my way by. If anyone's trapped in there, they're hurt, very badly, or they're dead. Feeling helpless, I glance back to the road. No sirens or flashing lights yet.

The first thing I see when I round the truck is a pair of enormous boots sticking out through the open door. I run over and climb up beside the boots to see inside the cab. A burly bear of a man is stretched out on the bench seat. Kate has her mouth over his. I watch his chest rise. She turns her head and puts her ear next to his mouth, noticing me in the open doorway. Putting her mouth over his, she gives him another breath.

Fingers pressed against his neck, she counts to ten. "He doesn't have a pulse, Pen. I think he had a heart attack." She places her overlapped hands on his chest. They look so small in comparison to the trucker's wide body. "Go see if Rick's back."

I hop down and run, my stomach aching like I've swallowed a pincushion. Rick comes sprinting down the highway, his arms a blur. We reach the car at the same time, and he nearly collapses in front of me, pointing at his chest.

"His inhaler!" Di rifles through the glove compartment. She jumps out of the car and hands it to him.

The faint wailing of sirens grows louder by the second. We stand back from the road and wait. Lights flashing, an ambulance, an EMT vehicle, and a police car swarm the scene, followed soon after by a green hatchback. A woman gets out of the car, her features stricken with panic. An officer gets out of his squad car and follows her as she hurries over to us.

"What happened?" she cries. "I was only gone an hour!"

"Ma'am, do you work here?" the officer asks.

"Yes. But I closed up and took an early lunch to visit a friend who had a baby last night." Over the roof of my car, she looks at the ruined fruit stand and bursts into tears.

The officer takes her by the arm and leads her to his car. I stand with Di and Rick, not knowing what we're supposed to be doing. A siren screams in the distance. In no time at all, a red fire-and-rescue truck rumbles toward us. From the other end of the highway, another police cruiser comes speeding in. There are a lot of people here now. Are all these people and trucks and cars and flashing colored lights necessary? I spin in a slow circle, taking everything in. I go back to standing still, but my head keeps on spinning.

One of the paramedics jogs over, scanning us from head to toe. "Hi, I'm Lisa," she says. "Come with me and I'll check you out."

"We didn't get in an accident," I try to explain. "My car pulled over before the truck went off the road. We're all okay."

Lisa tilts her head, staring at my arm. "Come on over anyway. I want to make sure."

We trail along behind her to the back of her vehicle.

"How'd you get those nasty scrapes?" Lisa says to me.

"My friend Kate and I were running up the road." I point out the gravel road. "And I slipped."

"You weren't in your car?"

Unable to stop myself from fidgeting, I say, "Um, no." I point to Di and Rick. "They were on their way back from town, and Kate and I decided to run out to meet them."

That sounds so moronic. I'm still damp from head to toe. As if Kate and I would choose to swim across the lake fully clothed and run up to the highway. Just for something to do. For fun! Lisa probably thinks I'm high on crack.

The ambulance that was attending to the trucker speeds off down the highway again.

Lisa washes and bandages my shredded arms, asking us lots of normal questions that don't seem to have anything to do with the accident. Everything about her is perky, her voice, her mannerisms, her nose, and her cute orange ponytail.

A police car pulls up beside us. In the front passenger seat sits Kate. She waves.

The officer gets out of the car, six feet of muscles packed into a uniform. "Your friend Kate is a hero."

Kate shrugs and rolls her eyes at us.

"Hey, how come you guys were soaking wet when you pulled us over?" Di asks, tugging on her bangs. "You didn't swim across the lake, did you?"

"We sure did," Kate declares, leaning out the window of the cruiser. "Emma dared us fifty bucks to do it, but Pen and

I were hot anyway. Pretty cool that we ended up being in the right place at the right time, isn't it. We must be psychic!"

I stare at Kate as she leans out the window of the cop car, a big gleaming smile on her dirty face, and I don't know whether to cry, burst out laughing, or both.

We ended up being in the right place at the right time. And this time, I wasn't too late.

When I woke up, I had a few spooky seconds where I honestly wondered if yesterday was just another one of my nightmares. But my bandages reminded me that yesterday was real, as did the dehydration hangover I woke up with. My tongue was like a dried loofah sponge.

"Here are your bacon and eggs," Mom says, placing a heaping plate of food on the table in front of Kate.

"Thanks so much, Penny's Mom."

Since the accident, Mom's been feeding us nonstop. I don't think she's cooked this much in the seventeen years I've known her.

"We're driving back to Kincardine this afternoon." I stab a fried potato with my fork.

"Oh, no, you're not," Mom says. "I called your father last night. He's coming to pick you up."

"What?" I guzzle my milk to dislodge the potato from my throat.

"You heard me. You're not driving that death trap. He's coming here to sell it."

Kate's hunched over her plate, shoveling in forkfuls of scrambled eggs. She raises her gaze to look at me, shrugs, and goes back to eating. So much for moral support.

"I barely even got to drive it, though," I whine. "All summer I used my own legs to get around, like a sucker."

"Uh huh," Mom says, buttering a row of hot toast.

"I didn't get to cruise around Kincardine with the windows down and the music cranked. That's a teenage rite of passage, Mom."

"Would you like some toast, Kate?" Mom says.

"I'd love some. Thanks."

I kick Kate under the table, prodding her to help me.

"I don't think your dad should sell the car either, Penny," she says in a stilted voice. "It's like a demented killer car out of a horror movie. Isn't that cool?"

Mom's glare strikes me between the eyes. "See? Kate agrees with me. The car goes."

After Kate and I finish eating, we do the dishes while Mom raids Super-Saver to restock her empty cupboards. I can barely dry the dishes without grimacing in pain. My arms and shoulders are fried, but my legs are even worse. All morning, I've been walking around like I don't have knees. Guess it's a good thing Dad's picking us up.

"Almost time to say good-bye to Rick and Di," Kate says.

"I'll call Di in a minute to say good-bye." I dry my hands on a dish towel. "I sure wish you could have met Ryan."

Scrubbing a plate, she says, "I will. Some other time."

ZZZ

Everybody in Dad's car is cloud-gazing. Kalli's seeing stuff like horses and castles and mermaids. Dad sees airplanes and turtles. Every cloud looks like food to Kate.

The clouds outside my window look like a big, soft, squishy mattress. I'd love to snuggle into it for a few days of dreamless comatose sleep. No dreams at all. Not even good ones. Just sleep.

"Kalli, can you turn the radio up?" Kate says.

Exaggerated rolling of the eyes. Check. Put-upon sigh. Check. Disgusted glance into the backseat. Check.

"It's a country song," she says.

"Where am I from?" Kate says. "Kincardine. Everybody in my hick town loves this music. It's inbred." With a squawk, Kate gives me a shove. "Get it? Hicks. Inbred."

The atrocious country song gets louder.

Kate slouches in her seat. Below the music, she says, "Think it'll bother you to see Di and Rick together?"

"I don't think so." My answer surprises me. But it's probably true. I loved the men Rick was before. I barely know him this time. "There's no way I could ever like him more than I like Ryan."

"You know, you should have let me keep the money Emma gave me." Kate shakes her head, smirking. "You big, honest jerk."

"Just because she had a hazy, pot-induced recollection of actually daring us fifty bucks to swim across the lake doesn't mean you get to take her money."

"Does too." She sticks her tongue out.

There's so much more I want to say to Kate that I don't know how I'd say it out loud. I open my bag and pull out my dream journal. On a page near the back, I write, *Can you imagine if I'd stayed home this summer?*

I hand the book and pen to Kate.

She hands it back with an answer scrawled beneath mine: *Mind-boggling, isn't it? Think about all you did!*

I cringe when I read the last sentence. The "you" part is all wrong. It wasn't me who succeeded. It was the two of us, together. We're a team. Getting choked up, I write, *What if I hadn't met you, Kate?*

The pen dangles from Kate's hand for a while as she decides what to write: *Ah, how quickly Psychic Penny forgets that I'm the one who suggested the trip home in the killer horror movie car in the first place.*

I stare at the empty space below her answer, unable to get what I want to say down on paper. The words are bumping around in my mind and slipping out of my grasp. I think about all the things Kate helped me with this summer. Geez. What if I hadn't met her?

Finally, I write a huge reply in only two words: *Thank you.*

She reads it and goes back to staring at clouds. After a few minutes, I feel the book slide onto my lap. It reads, *No problem.*

When I look over at Kate, I catch her in the midst of wiping her eyes with the back of her hand. I give her a perplexed look, and she snatches the book off my lap again.

What? I've got an eyelash in my eye!!

18

Dear Dream Journal:

Could this be my very last journal entry? I'll probably continue to use you, even if I don't have any psychotic dreams to record. I'm kind of attached to you now.

We returned to Kincardine in time for their weeklong summer festival, complete with a Highland Games competition, fish dinners in a gigantic tent at the beach, a beach dance, and two Pipe Band parades. I thought I'd died and gone to Scottish heaven. It was the most fun I've ever had. And Kate met a guy. A sweet, not to mention extremely good looking, guy named Owen, from a neighboring town, who she had an instant connection with. It was almost like they'd met before, she told me.

This morning, Dad drove Kalli and me home. It was so tough to leave my beach, my cottage, my dog Sandy, and Kate. As we were loading up Dad's car, Kate came over to say good-bye, and I started crying. I couldn't help it. I'll really miss our jogs and late-night beach talks. She gave me a hug (not before smacking me in the arm first, of course) and reminded me that I'll be back at the cottage for Christmas. I don't think I'll last that long. I foresee many weekend visits to Dad's place in my future.

As much as I loved my time at Dad's, I am happy to be home. When I stepped in the door, I felt like I'd been holding my breath the whole time I was away and I could finally exhale. Sure, I may be a pro at holding my breath, but two months is a long time.

Ryan is on his way over at this very minute. I don't know how I'll react when he gets here, and that makes me nervous. Guess I should get going.

I close my journal and set it on my nightstand. In front of the bathroom mirror, I run a brush through my hair and spritz some body spray down my shirt. They should make a full-body deodorant for sweaty, nervous people. I sure could use some right now.

I head downstairs to wait.

As I'm opening the fridge to get a snack, somebody knocks on the back door. I listen for Sandy's woof. When it doesn't come, I bite down on my lip, not wanting to wreck this happy moment with tears. I run into the laundry room. Ryan and I stare at each other with the screen door between us. He smiles, and that's all it takes to relax me. He comes inside and wraps his arms around me. His tight squeeze lifts me right off the floor.

He sets me down and steps back to look at me. "Wow."

"What's the matter?"

"Nothing's the matter," he says. "You just look different."

Different good or different bad? "I do?"

"You look like a Roman goddess."

That makes me laugh. If I'd known jogging would make me look like a goddess, I would have taken it up years ago.

"C'mon in. Kalli's at a friend's place and Mom isn't home from work yet. We can go up to my room and talk."

Probably assuming that "talk" is a code word for something else, Ryan grabs my hand. We hurry through the kitchen and up the stairs.

I take the manila envelope of photos out of my bag. "Here are the pictures from my modeling shoot."

The stack of photos slides out onto Ryan's large palm. On top sits the vignette photo of Kate and me. "This is Kate?" he asks, squinting at the picture.

"Yeah," I say. I wish I were a kid so I could bounce on the bed and not look moronic.

"She looks familiar. I can't think of who she looks like." He studies that picture for a while, shrugs, and goes through the rest of the photos. "Those are great," he says, getting back to the vignette. "Can I have the one of you peeking through the monkey bars?"

"Sure."

"Penny, are you here?" Mom calls. Before I have time to answer, she's pounding up the stairs. She bursts through the doorway and throws her arms wide. "Get over here."

I give her a loose hug. "Mom, you saw me two weeks ago."

"I know, but I missed you lots in those two weeks. And how's my Kate?"

"The same. She's good."

"I brought a bucket of fried chicken home for dinner," Mom says. "Come downstairs. Ryan, you're staying to eat with us."

"Okay."

"I'm so happy you're back home." Mom gives me another hug, putting her mouth to my ear. "No boys in your bedroom." Loosening her grip, she says, "Let's go eat. The chicken is getting cold."

Ryan stands to follow her, but I grab his arm and we hang back. The sound of clattering plates and silverware in the kitchen signals that we can dive into each other's arms for a hug without getting busted by Mom. I stand on my tiptoes and snuggle my face into the soft spot between his shoulder and his neck. We fit together perfectly. I could stay in Ryan's hug forever. He tilts his head and gives me a kiss. I kiss him back.

At the exact second our kissing starts to pick up steam, Mom shouts, "Food's ready!"

We separate before our hug gets hot enough to set off the smoke alarm.

Ryan clears his throat. "Guess we should go down there."

I grab the pile of photos, return them to the envelope, and stick it back in my bag. When I stand, a colorful business card is right in front of my face, tacked to my message board. It catches my attention like a billboard sign. Mom must have put it there while I was gone. I take it down and look it over.

Margie's info is on the front. And on the back is a note. *Penny,
please don't hesitate to call if you meet "you-know-who."*

"I'll be down in a minute," I tell Ryan. "I have to call
somebody."

He smiles at me as he leaves the room and nearly bonks
into the door frame.

I stare at the card in disbelief. Margie remembers me. She
even remembers the reading she gave me. The reading that
turned out to be accurate after all.

When Ryan's jogging footsteps reach the bottom of the
stairs, I pick up the phone and dial the number on the card.
Margie's husky voice answers. Too afraid to open my big
mouth for once, I need to remind myself that she wouldn't have
given me the card if she didn't expect me to call.

"Um, hi, this is Penny Fitzsimmons."

"Penny, it's nice to hear from you. Did you meet him? Is
that why you're calling?"

"Yes, I met him," I say. "He's my friend Diana's new
boyfriend."

"I see."

Uncomfortable silence.

"Margie, did you know that Diana and Ulrich, the boy you
told me about, were supposed to die in a car accident? Did you
see that at my mom's party?"

"No, I didn't. But I did see fire around them," she says. "I
take it you discovered some interesting things about yourself
this summer, Penny?"

"I know why you asked me if I'd ever tried to psychically read someone," I stammer.

"I see. You prevented the accident?"

"Yes, my friend Kate and I did."

"That's wonderful. Congratulations."

"Thanks," I say. "I have a question, though. I'm not sure if I did everything I was supposed to do. Was stopping the car accident enough?" *Can you whip out a crystal ball, look forward in time, and make sure we're all okay?* "I understand that I had to give up the guy I was destined to be with forever—"

"Hold on now, back up the cart," Margie says, interrupting me. "I didn't say he was the person you were destined to be with forever. I asked if you believe in destiny."

"Oh."

"A thousand years ago, you made a mistake, and it's haunted you through every lifetime since," Margie says. "You changed your friends' fates this summer. But did you consider that fixing the mistake from your past would change your fate, too?"

Once again, somebody's pointing out my pathetic reasoning skills. "No, not really."

"Hon, you didn't just help your friends. You also helped yourself."

I lean back against the wall, slowly absorbing Margie's words. *I helped myself?*

"At your mom's party, I told you you've been in love with Ulrich for the last thousand years." Margie pauses. A match ignites with a sizzling crack. Her lips withdraw from her cigarette with a soft *puh,* and she exhales a lazy stream of smoke into the phone. "But, honey, I never said anything about the thousand years before that."

I close my eyes, almost able to smell mint.

"You think about that, Penny," she says. "I'll talk to you soon."

"Okay, I will. Bye."

I hang up and leave my room, bewildered. Margie just told me something important, I'm sure of it. And if my brain wasn't such a ghost town, I'm sure I could figure it out. Where's Kate when I need her?

When I get to the bottom of the stairs, I come to a sudden stop. The entranceway to the kitchen is framing a clear shot of Ryan, who's seated at the kitchen table, and Di and Rick, who are standing in the laundry room, like they're in a photo together. This is the first time I've seen my past-life boyfriend and my real boyfriend in the same room.

Ryan turns around on his chair. "Hi, Di. What's up, Legs?"

"Nothing much, Fly-man," Rick says, like the Legs comment made sense to him.

"You guys know each other?" I say, coming into the kitchen.

"From our swim team." Ryan searches through the bucket of chicken and pulls out a drumstick. "We didn't know that we both knew Di, until she came to our last meet."

"Isn't it great that our boyfriends are friends?" Di says.

I force myself to smile. I think I need to sit down. I pull out the chair beside Ryan.

"Do you guys want something to eat?" I ask, even though I know I couldn't pay Di to eat fried chicken.

They sit across the table from us, but Di says, "No, thanks. We're eating later."

The three of them start talking about swimming and people I don't know. Di must have become a swim groupie while I was gone, because she's throwing lingo around like she's an expert. My attention slips from listening to them. I go over what Margie told me on the phone.

A thousand years ago, I made a mistake, she said. She must have been talking about the Viking dreams. There's a start. I'll run with that.

I study the blue-and-white checks in my placemat, running nowhere fast. Dusty tumbleweeds blow through town, but I clear them away and focus.

It's our thousand-year reunion. That leads me to think of Kate. My finger taps down four squares in the placemat, making a checklist. Di and I were in the dreams, with Leif and Raven. But there's someone missing. I tap through the squares one more time. The tip of my finger hovers above the fifth square.

Kate had asked, "Who's Raven?" Maybe equally important, is the question she didn't ask.

Who is Erik?

I frantically try to recall those dreams, to see my journal

entries in my mind. The dream at the river, with the boys play-ing in the water, we were all in that one. And then, right before I woke up, Ryan eagerly jumped out to ask me if I wanted to watch a movie. It made me angry that he was blocking my view of Leif.

I swallow hard, as the familiar feather dusters roll down my body. That wasn't the only time I dreamed of Ryan. My mind flashes to an image of him withdrawing into a dark forest. I see the sadness in his face. Pushing myself to remember, I attach the image to the dream I had about Raven leaving me. Di and Rick jumped. And Erik drowned.

I thought I'd never actually seen Erik in any of the dreams. He was a name, nothing more. Was he there all along?

You made a mistake. It's haunted you through every lifetime since. I didn't say anything about the thousand years before that.

"Hellooo?" Di waves her hand in front of my face. "Earth to Penny."

I pull out of deep thought, but it's difficult, like climbing out of quicksand I actually want to sink into. "What?"

"I asked you who you want to win."

"Win what?"

Di sighs. "What we've been talking about for the past five minutes. The guys have a bet going, to see who can get the best time in the 200-yard butterfly." She lays her head on Rick's shoulder. "Personally, I think Rick's going to blow Ryan out of the water." Her hair works its magic, along with a smile. "No offense, Ryan."

Ryan and I turn to look at each other at the same time. My gaze twirls through the soft curls he's grown over the summer and brushes across the fading pinkness of his sunburned cheeks. I study the new freckles on his nose and the one slightly crooked tooth that makes his smile interesting. It's like I'm really seeing him for the first time. How could I have been so blind?

I take hold of my boyfriend's hand under the table. "Sorry, Di. But I'm going to have to choose Ryan."

And it only took me a thousand years to say that.